MW01364249

THE TOLKIEN DIARY 1995

ILLUSTRATED BY JOHN HOWE

HarperCollins*Publishers*

HarperCollins*Publishers*
77-85 Fulham Palace Road
Hammersmith, London W6 8JB

Published by HarperCollins*Publishers* 1994
The Lord of The Rings Diary 1995

ISBN 0261 10309 1

Printed in Hong Kong

JOHN RONALD REUEL TOLKIEN was born on 3rd January 1892 in Bloemfontein in the Orange Free State. He was educated at King Edward's School, Birmingham where he began to develop his linguistic talent.

1914 saw the outbreak of the First World War. Tolkien graduated in 1915 with a first in English language and literature at Oxford. Before embarking for France in 1916, he married his childhood sweetheart, Edith Bratt. He survived the Somme, but was later invalided home.

After the war Tolkien became Professor of Anglo-Saxon at Oxford. He had already started writing the great cycle of myths that became *The Silmarillion*. He and Edith had four children and it was for them that he first told the tale of *The Hobbit* which was published in 1937. It was so successful that the publishers instantly wanted a sequel, but it was not until 1954 that the first volume of his great masterpiece, *The Lord of the Rings*, appeared. Its enormous popularity took Tolkien by surprise.

After retirement Ronald and Edith Tolkien moved to Bournemouth where Edith died in 1971. Tolkien then returned to Oxford. He died in 1973.

JOHN HOWE was born in 1957 in Vancouver, Canada. After finishing High School, he moved to France in 1976. He attended the Ecole des Arts Décoratifs de Strasbourg, where he gained a Diploma in Illustration in 1981. He currently lives in Switzerland with his wife, Fataneh, who is also an illustrator, and his five year old son, Dana. He has illustrated many French children's books, as well as editions of *Rip Van Winkle* and *Jack and the Beanstalk* for a publisher in Boston.

John Howe's work has featured in several of the highly successful Tolkien Calendars, in posters commemorating the 50th anniversary of the publication of *The Hobbit* and the centenary of Tolkien's birth, and on the jackets and covers of the HarperCollins centenary editions of *The Hobbit*, *The Lord of the Rings* and *The Silmarillion*.

He writes 'Somewhat shamefacedly, I am obliged to admit that I first read *The Two Towers* and *The Return of the King*, and finally *The Fellowship of the Ring*. I believe I was twelve or so at the time (I had read *The Hobbit* several years before), and the road to higher fantasy was only to be reached through the shelves of the small town public library. Thus I plunged directly into the world of Tolkien just above the Falls of Rauros and have been swimming diligently ever since.'

C·A·L·E·N·D·A·R

1994

	JANUARY	*FEBRUARY*	*MARCH*	*APRIL*	*MAY*	*JUNE*
M	3 10 17 24 31	7 14 21 28	7 14 21 28	4 11 18 25	2 9 16 23 30	6 13 20 27
T	4 11 18 25	1 8 15 22	1 8 15 22 29	5 12 19 26	3 10 17 24 31	7 14 21 28
W	5 12 19 26	2 9 16 23	2 9 16 23 30	6 13 20 27	4 11 18 25	1 8 15 22 29
T	6 13 20 27	3 10 17 24	3 10 17 24 31	7 14 21 28	5 12 19 26	2 9 16 23 30
F	7 14 21 28	4 11 18 25	4 11 18 25	1 8 15 22 29	6 13 20 27	3 10 17 24
S	1 8 15 22 29	5 12 19 26	5 12 19 26	2 9 16 23 30	7 14 21 28	4 11 18 25
S	2 9 16 23 30	6 13 20 27	6 13 20 27	3 10 17 24	1 8 15 22 29	5 12 19 26

	JULY	*AUGUST*	*SEPTEMBER*	*OCTOBER*	*NOVEMBER*	*DECEMBER*
M	4 11 18 25	1 8 15 22 29	5 12 19 26	3 10 17 24 31	7 14 21 28	5 12 19 26
T	5 12 19 26	2 9 16 23 30	6 13 20 27	4 11 18 25	1 8 15 22 29	6 13 20 27
W	6 13 20 27	3 10 17 24 31	7 14 21 28	5 12 19 26	2 9 16 23 30	7 14 21 28
T	7 14 21 28	4 11 18 25	1 8 15 22 29	6 13 20 27	3 10 17 24	1 8 15 22 29
F	1 8 15 22 29	5 12 19 26	2 9 16 23 30	7 14 21 28	4 11 18 25	2 9 16 23 30
S	2 9 16 23 30	6 13 20 27	3 10 17 24	1 8 15 22 29	5 12 19 26	3 10 17 24 31
S	3 10 17 24 31	7 14 21 28	4 11 18 25	2 9 16 23 30	6 13 20 27	4 11 18 25

1996

	JANUARY	*FEBRUARY*	*MARCH*	*APRIL*	*MAY*	*JUNE*
M	1 8 15 22 29	5 12 19 26	4 11 18 25	1 8 15 22 29	6 13 20 27	3 10 17 24
T	2 9 16 23 30	6 13 20 27	5 12 19 26	2 9 16 23 30	7 14 21 28	4 11 18 25
W	3 10 17 24 31	7 14 21 28	6 13 20 27	3 10 17 24	1 8 15 22 29	5 12 19 26
T	4 11 18 25	1 8 15 22 29	7 14 21 28	4 11 18 25	2 9 16 23 30	6 13 20 27
F	5 12 19 26	2 9 16 23	1 8 15 22 29	5 12 19 26	3 10 17 24 31	7 14 21 28
S	6 13 20 27	3 10 17 24	2 9 16 23 30	6 13 20 27	4 11 18 25	1 8 15 22 29
S	7 14 21 28	4 11 18 25	3 10 17 24 31	7 14 21 28	5 12 19 26	2 9 16 23 30

	JULY	*AUGUST*	*SEPTEMBER*	*OCTOBER*	*NOVEMBER*	*DECEMBER*
M	1 8 15 22 29	5 12 19 26	2 9 16 23 30	7 14 21 28	4 11 18 25	2 9 16 23 30
T	2 9 16 23 30	6 13 20 27	3 10 17 24	1 8 15 22 29	5 12 19 26	3 10 17 24 31
W	3 10 17 24 31	7 14 21 28	4 11 18 25	2 9 16 23 30	6 13 20 27	4 11 18 25
T	4 11 18 25	1 8 15 22 29	5 12 19 26	3 10 17 24 31	7 14 21 28	5 12 19 26
F	5 12 19 26	2 9 16 23 30	6 13 20 27	4 11 18 25	1 8 15 22 29	6 13 20 27
S	6 13 20 27	3 10 17 24 31	7 14 21 28	5 12 19 26	2 9 16 23 30	7 14 21 28
S	7 14 21 28	4 11 18 25	1 8 15 22 29	6 13 20 27	3 10 17 24	1 8 15 22 29

C·A·L·E·N·D·A·R

1995

JANUARY						
M		2	9	16	23	30
T		3	10	17	24	31
W		4	11	18	25	
T		5	12	19	26	
F		6	13	20	27	
S		7	14	21	28	
S	1	8	15	22	29	

FEBRUARY					
M		6	13	20	27
T		7	14	21	28
W	1	8	15	22	
T	2	9	16	23	
F	3	10	17	24	
S	4	11	18	25	
S	5	12	19	26	

MARCH					
M		6	13	20	27
T		7	14	21	28
W	1	8	15	22	29
T	2	9	16	23	30
F	3	10	17	24	31
S	4	11	18	25	
S	5	12	19	26	

APRIL					
M		3	10	17	24
T		4	11	18	25
W		5	12	19	26
T		6	13	20	27
F		7	14	21	28
S	1	8	15	22	29
S	2	9	16	23	30

MAY					
M	1	8	15	22	29
T	2	9	16	23	30
W	3	10	17	24	31
T	4	11	18	25	
F	5	12	19	26	
S	6	13	20	27	
S	7	14	21	28	

JUNE					
M		5	12	19	26
T		6	13	20	27
W		7	14	21	28
T	1	8	15	22	29
F	2	9	16	23	30
S	3	10	17	24	
S	4	11	18	25	

JULY						
M		3	10	17	24	31
T		4	11	18	25	
W		5	12	19	26	
T		6	13	20	27	
F		7	14	21	28	
S	1	8	15	22	29	
S	2	9	16	23	30	

AUGUST					
M		7	14	21	28
T	1	8	15	22	29
W	2	9	16	23	30
T	3	10	17	24	31
F	4	11	18	25	
S	5	12	19	26	
S	6	13	20	27	

SEPTEMBER					
M		4	11	18	25
T		5	12	19	26
W		6	13	20	27
T		7	14	21	28
F	1	8	15	22	29
S	2	9	16	23	30
S	3	10	17	24	

OCTOBER						
M		2	9	16	23	30
T		3	10	17	24	31
W		4	11	18	25	
T		5	12	19	26	
F		6	13	20	27	
S		7	14	21	28	
S	1	8	15	22	29	

NOVEMBER					
M		6	13	20	27
T		7	14	21	28
W	1	8	15	22	29
T	2	9	16	23	30
F	3	10	17	24	
S	4	11	18	25	
S	5	12	19	26	

DECEMBER						
M		4	11	18	25	
T		5	12	19	26	
W		6	13	20	27	
T		7	14	21	28	
F	1	8	15	22	29	
S	2	9	16	23	30	
S	3	10	17	24	31	

PUBLIC HOLIDAYS

Good Friday .... *Friday April 14*
Easter Monday .... *Monday April 17*
Christmas Day .... *Monday December 25*

UNITED KINGDOM

New Year's Day .... *Sunday January 1*
Bank Holiday .... *Monday January 2*
Bank Holiday (Scotland) .... *Tuesday January 3*
May Day Holiday .... *Monday May 1*
Spring Bank Holiday .... *Monday May 29*
Orangeman's Day (Northern Ireland) .... *Wednesday July 12*
Summer Bank Holiday (Scotland) .... *Monday August 7*
Summer Bank Holiday (England, Wales and Northern Ireland) .... *Monday August 28*
Boxing Day Holiday .... *Tuesday December 26*

REPUBLIC OF IRELAND

St Patrick's Day .... *Friday March 17*
St Stephen's Day .... *Tuesday December 26*

UNITED STATES OF AMERICA

Martin Luther King Day .... *Monday January 16*
Washington's Birthday Holiday .... *Monday February 20*
Memorial Day .... *Monday May 29*
Independence Day Holiday .... *Tuesday July 4*
Labor Day .... *Monday September 4*
Columbus Day .... *Monday October 9*
Veteran's Day .... *Friday November 10*
Thanksgiving Day .... *Thursday November 23*
New Year Holiday .... *Monday January 2*

CANADA

New Year's Day Holiday .... *Monday January 2*
Victoria Day .... *Monday May 22*
Canada Day .... *Monday July 3*
Labour Day .... *Monday September 4*
Thanksgiving Day .... *Monday October 9*
Remembrance Day .... *Monday November 13*
Christmas Day Holiday .... *Monday December 25*
Boxing Day Holiday .... *Tuesday December 26*

AUSTRALIA AND NEW ZEALAND

New Year's Day Holiday .... *Monday January 2*
Australia Day (Australia) .... *Thursday January 26*
Anzac Day .... *Tuesday April 25*
Labour Day (New Zealand) .... *Monday October 23*
Christmas Day Holiday .... *Monday December 25*
Boxing Day Holiday .... *Tuesday December 26*

D·E·C·E·M·B·E·R

26 *Monday*

27 *Tuesday*

28 *Wednesday*

29 *Thursday*

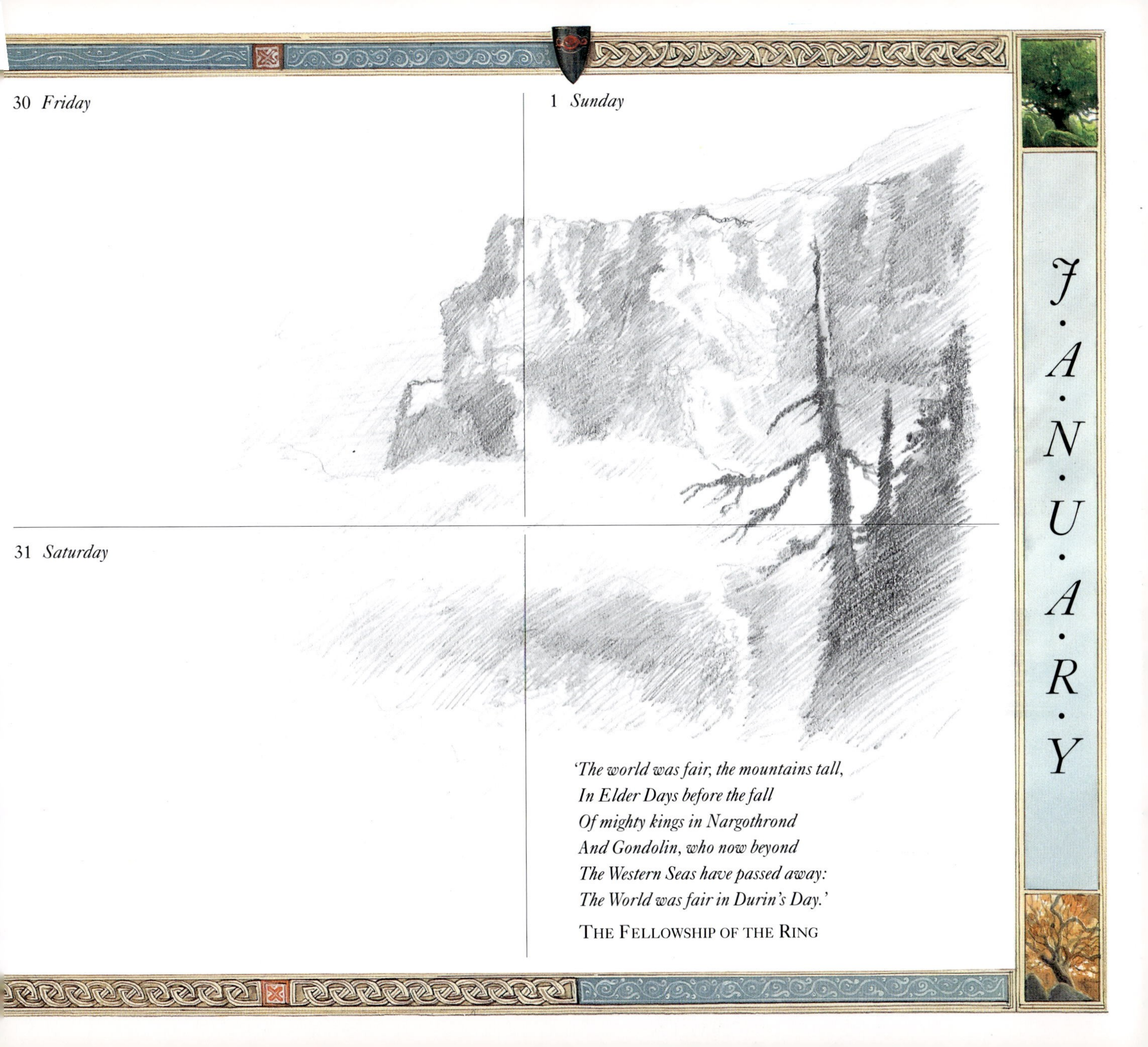

30 *Friday*

1 *Sunday*

31 *Saturday*

JANUARY

'The world was fair, the mountains tall,
In Elder Days before the fall
Of mighty kings in Nargothrond
And Gondolin, who now beyond
The Western Seas have passed away:
The World was fair in Durin's Day.'

THE FELLOWSHIP OF THE RING

J·A·N·U·A·R·Y

2 *Monday*

3 *Tuesday*

On 3rd January 1892 John Ronald Reuel Tolkien was born in Bloemfontein.

4 *Wednesday*

5 *Thursday*

THE COMPANY OF THE RING APPROACHING CARADHRAS

J·A·N·U·A·R·Y

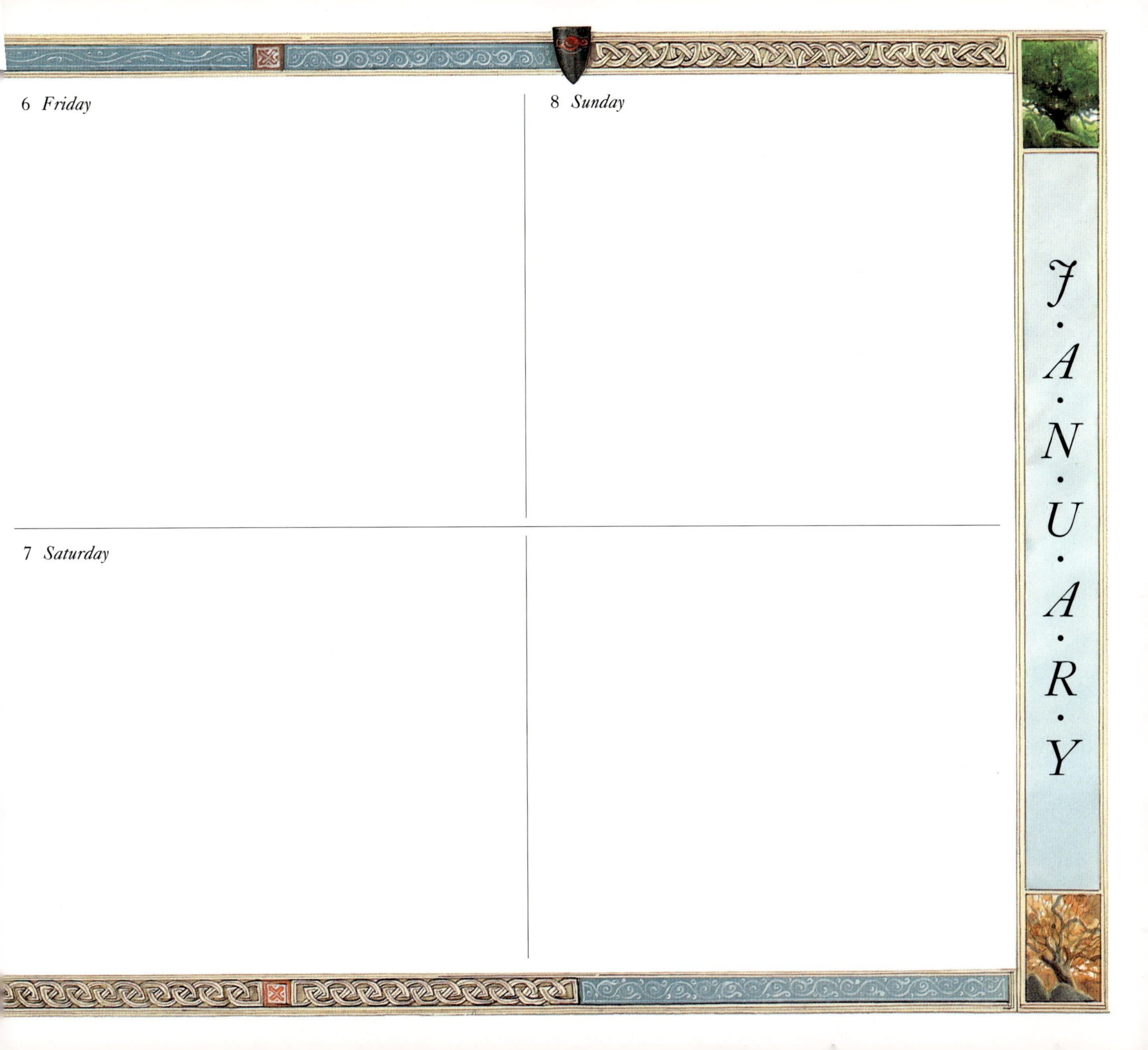

6 *Friday*

8 *Sunday*

7 *Saturday*

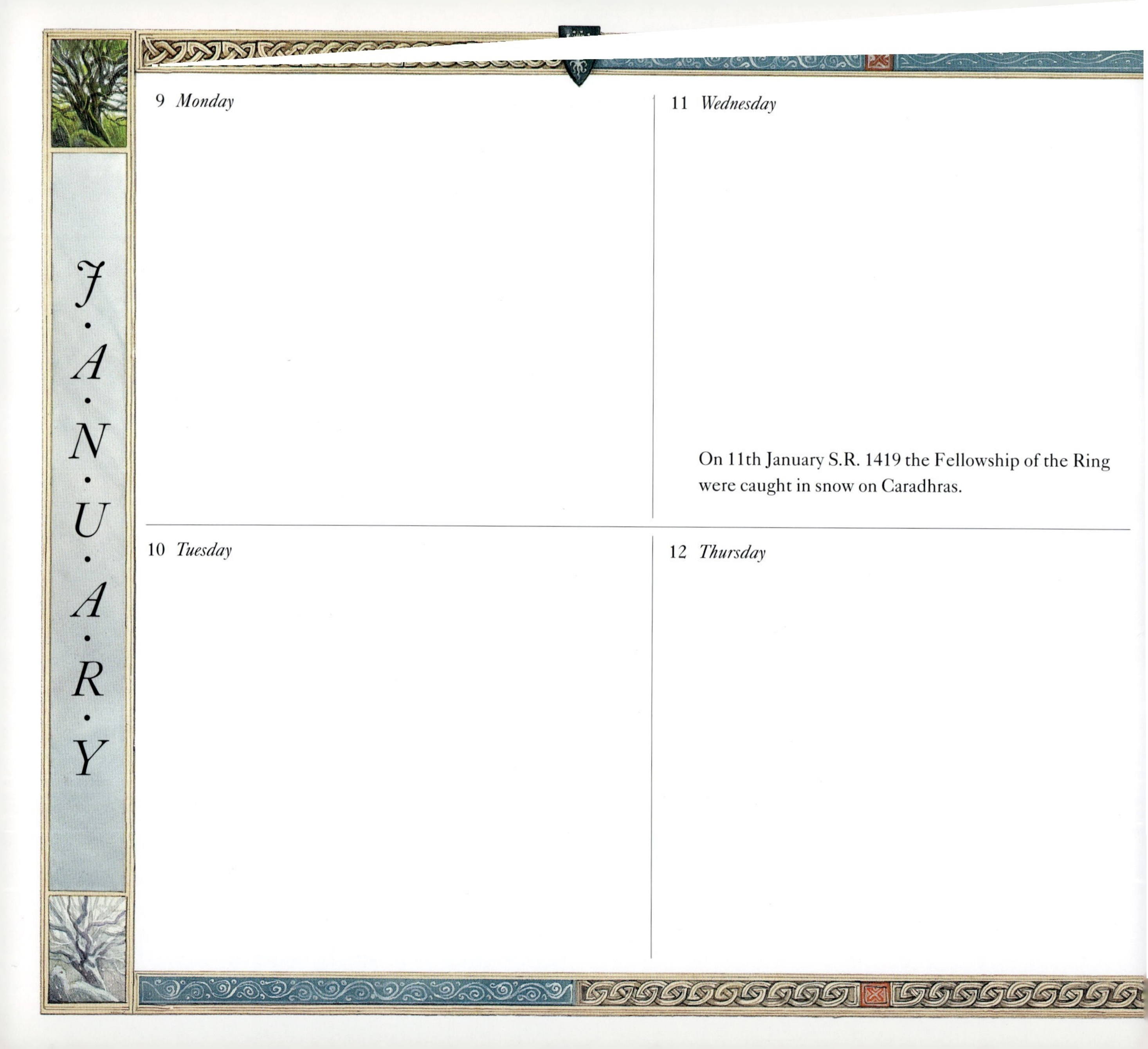

J·A·N·U·A·R·Y

9 *Monday*

10 *Tuesday*

11 *Wednesday*

On 11th January S.R. 1419 the Fellowship of the Ring were caught in snow on Caradhras.

12 *Thursday*

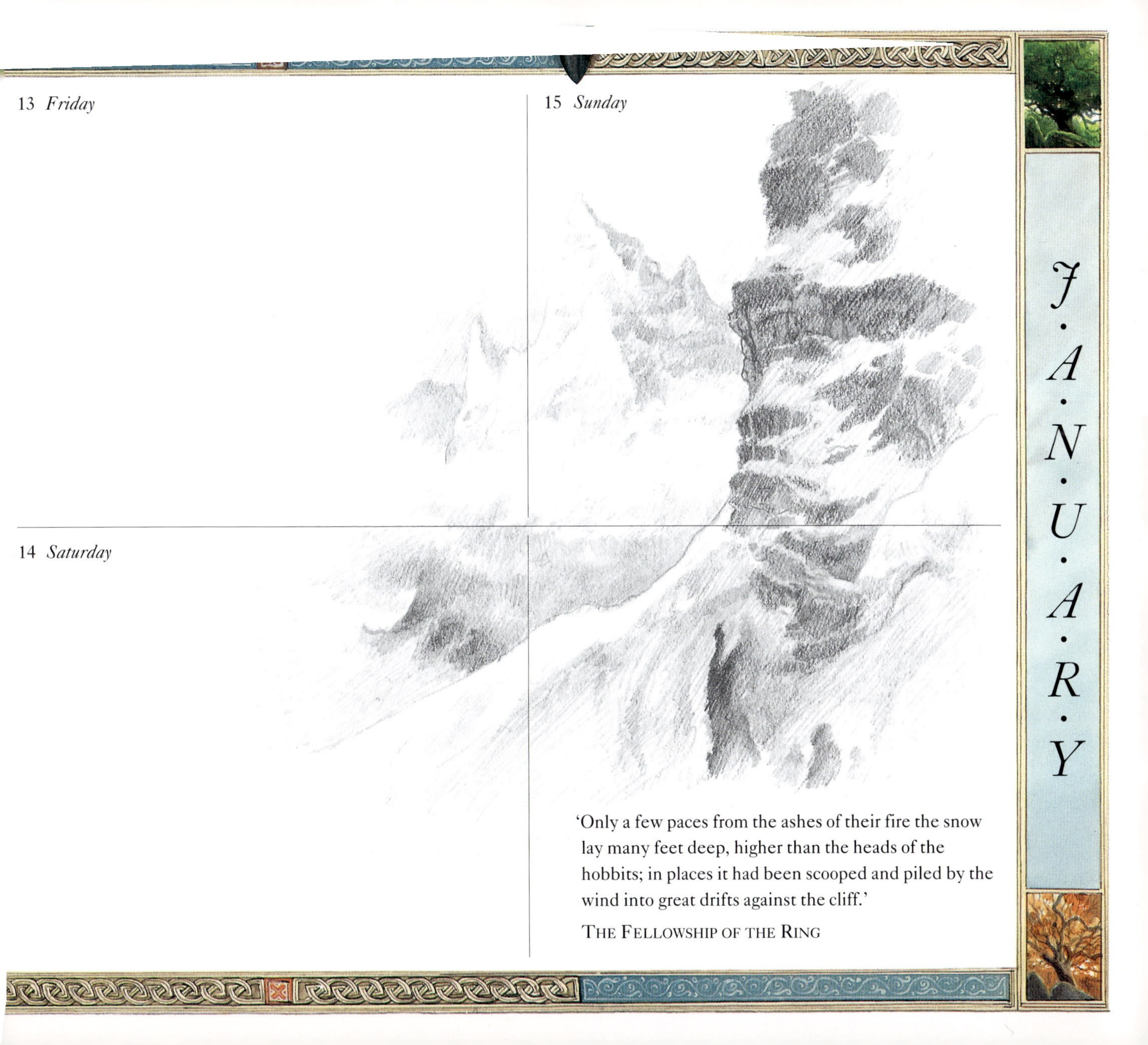

13 *Friday*

15 *Sunday*

14 *Saturday*

'Only a few paces from the ashes of their fire the snow lay many feet deep, higher than the heads of the hobbits; in places it had been scooped and piled by the wind into great drifts against the cliff.'

THE FELLOWSHIP OF THE RING

16 *Monday*

17 *Tuesday*

18 *Wednesday*

19 *Thursday*

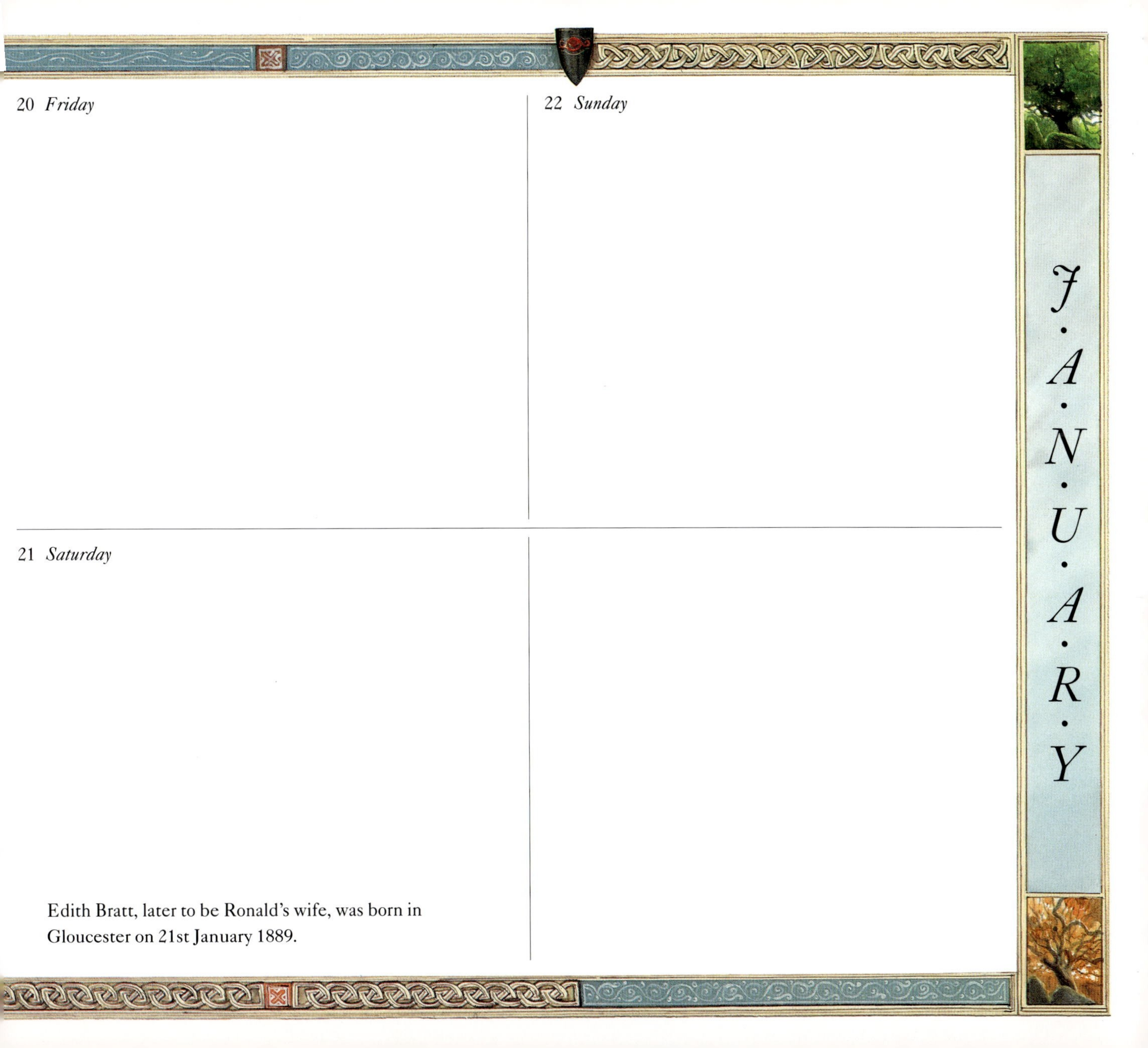

20 *Friday*

21 *Saturday*

Edith Bratt, later to be Ronald's wife, was born in Gloucester on 21st January 1889.

22 *Sunday*

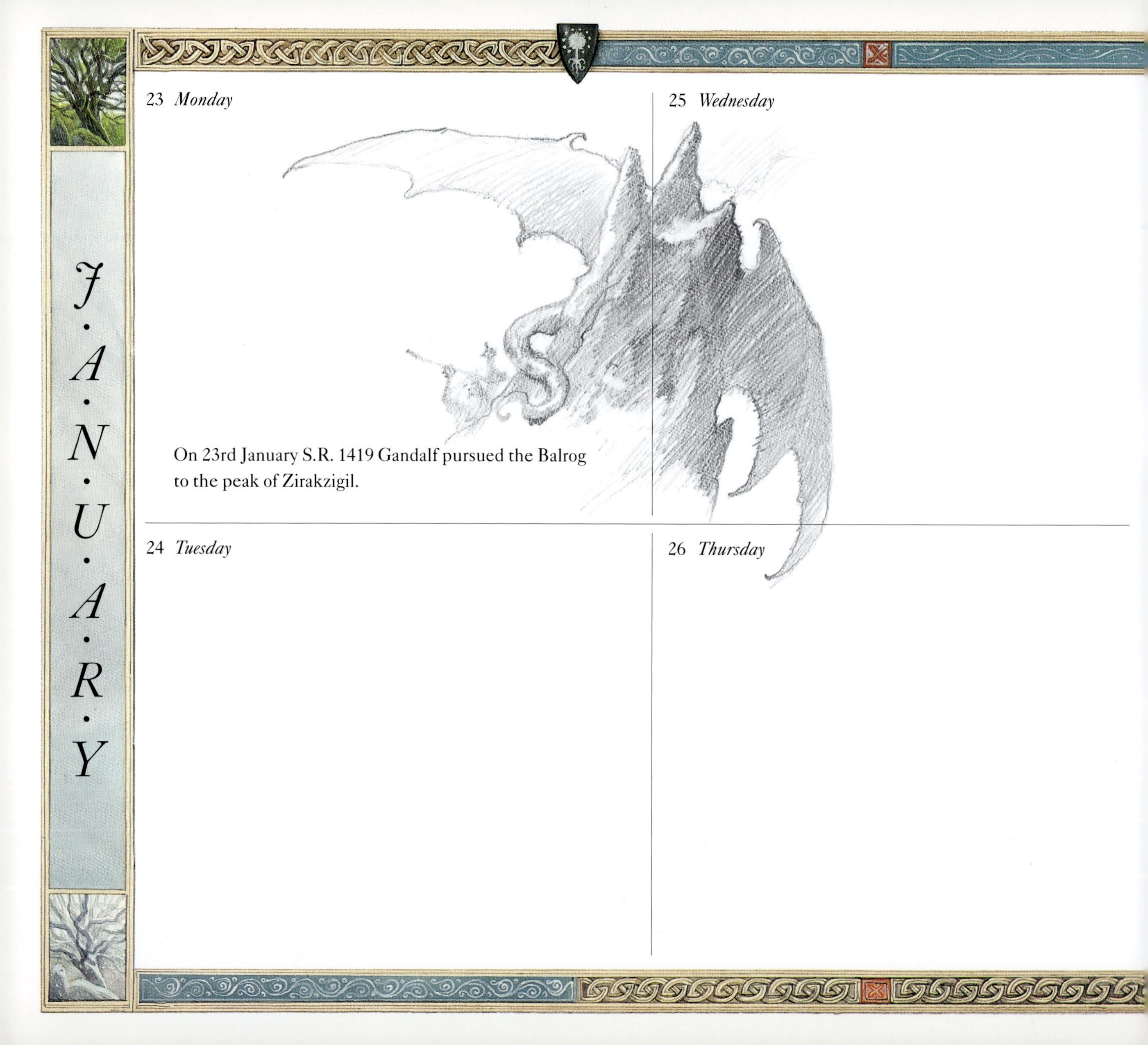

J·A·N·U·A·R·Y

23 *Monday*

On 23rd January S.R. 1419 Gandalf pursued the Balrog to the peak of Zirakzigil.

24 *Tuesday*

25 *Wednesday*

26 *Thursday*

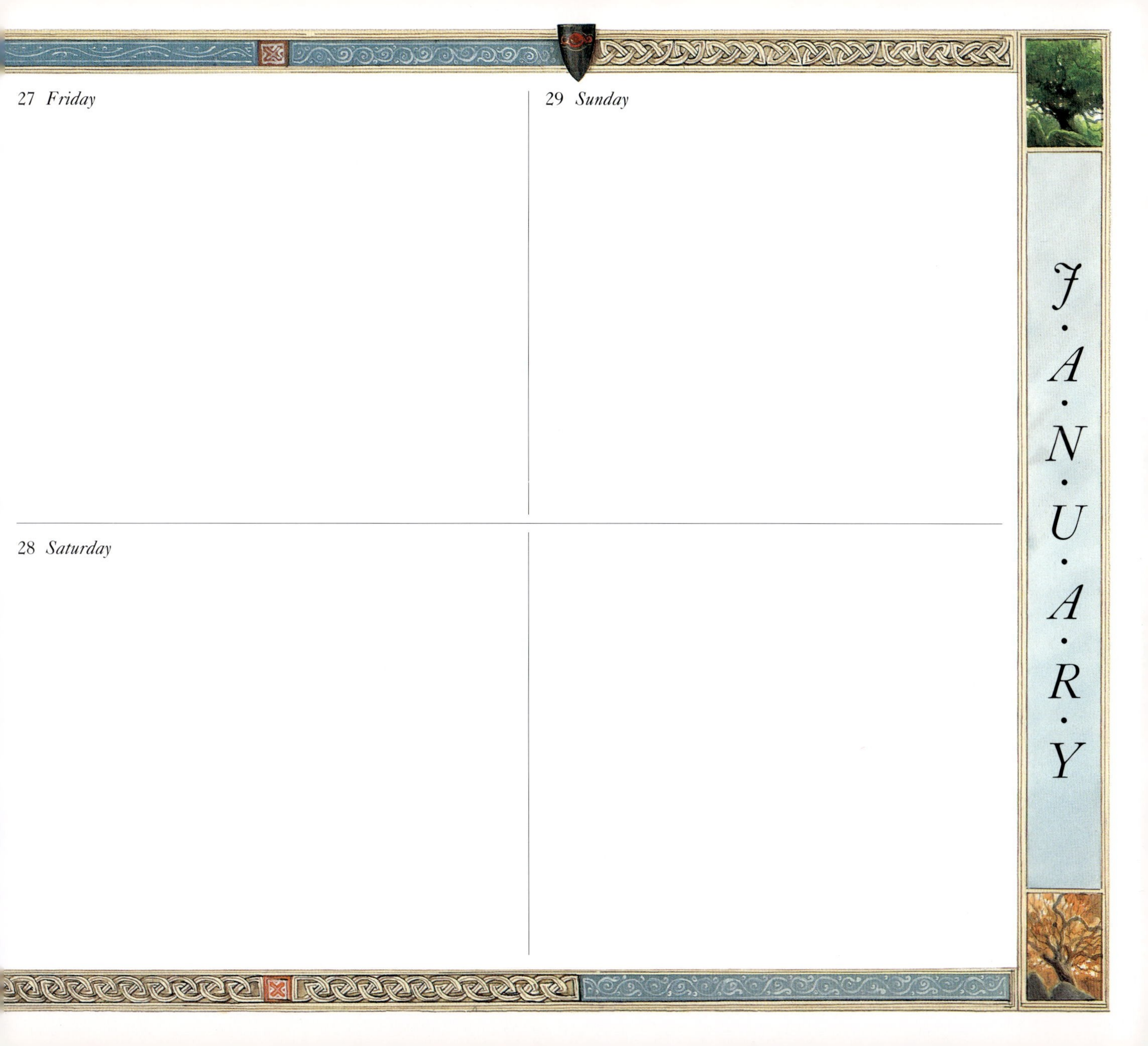
27 Friday
29 Sunday
28 Saturday
J·A·N·U·A·R·Y

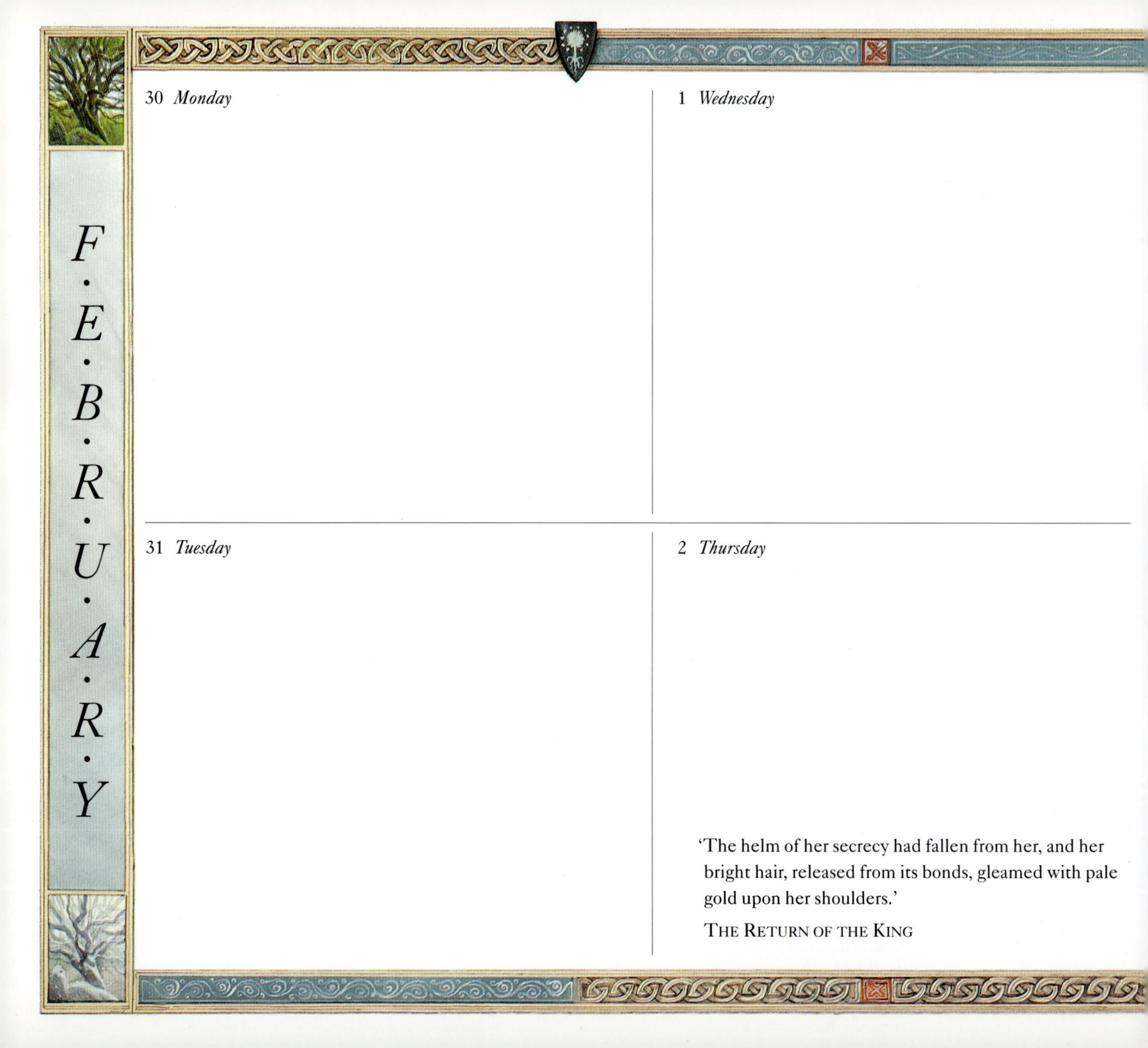

30 *Monday*

31 *Tuesday*

1 *Wednesday*

2 *Thursday*

'The helm of her secrecy had fallen from her, and her bright hair, released from its bonds, gleamed with pale gold upon her shoulders.'

THE RETURN OF THE KING

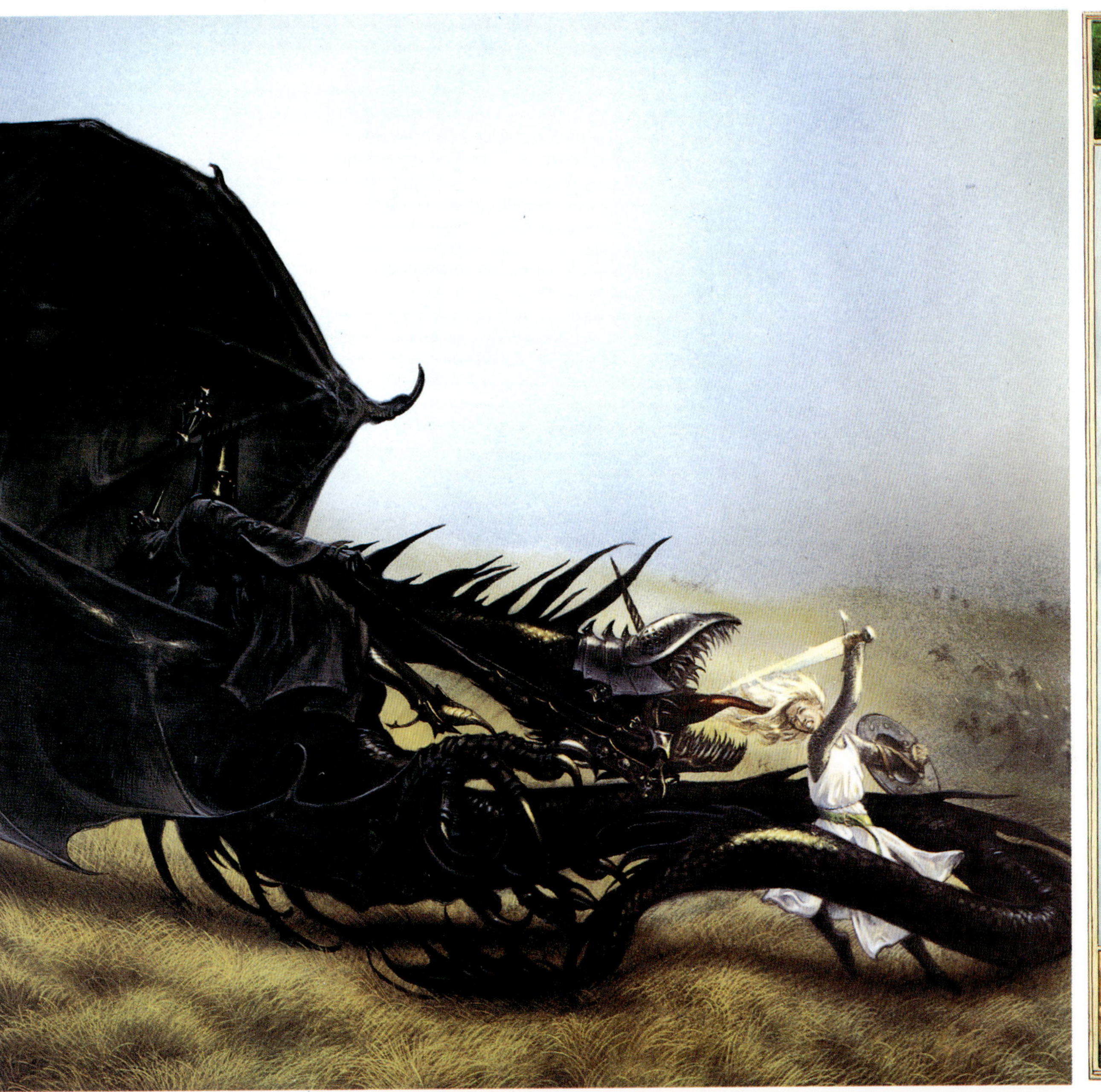

F·E·B·R·U·A·R·Y

3 *Friday*

5 *Sunday*

4 *Saturday*

F·E·B·R·U·A·R·Y

F·E·B·R·U·A·R·Y
6 Monday
8 Wednesday
7 Tuesday
9 Thursday

10 *Friday*

12 *Sunday*

11 *Saturday*

F·E·B·R·U·A·R·Y

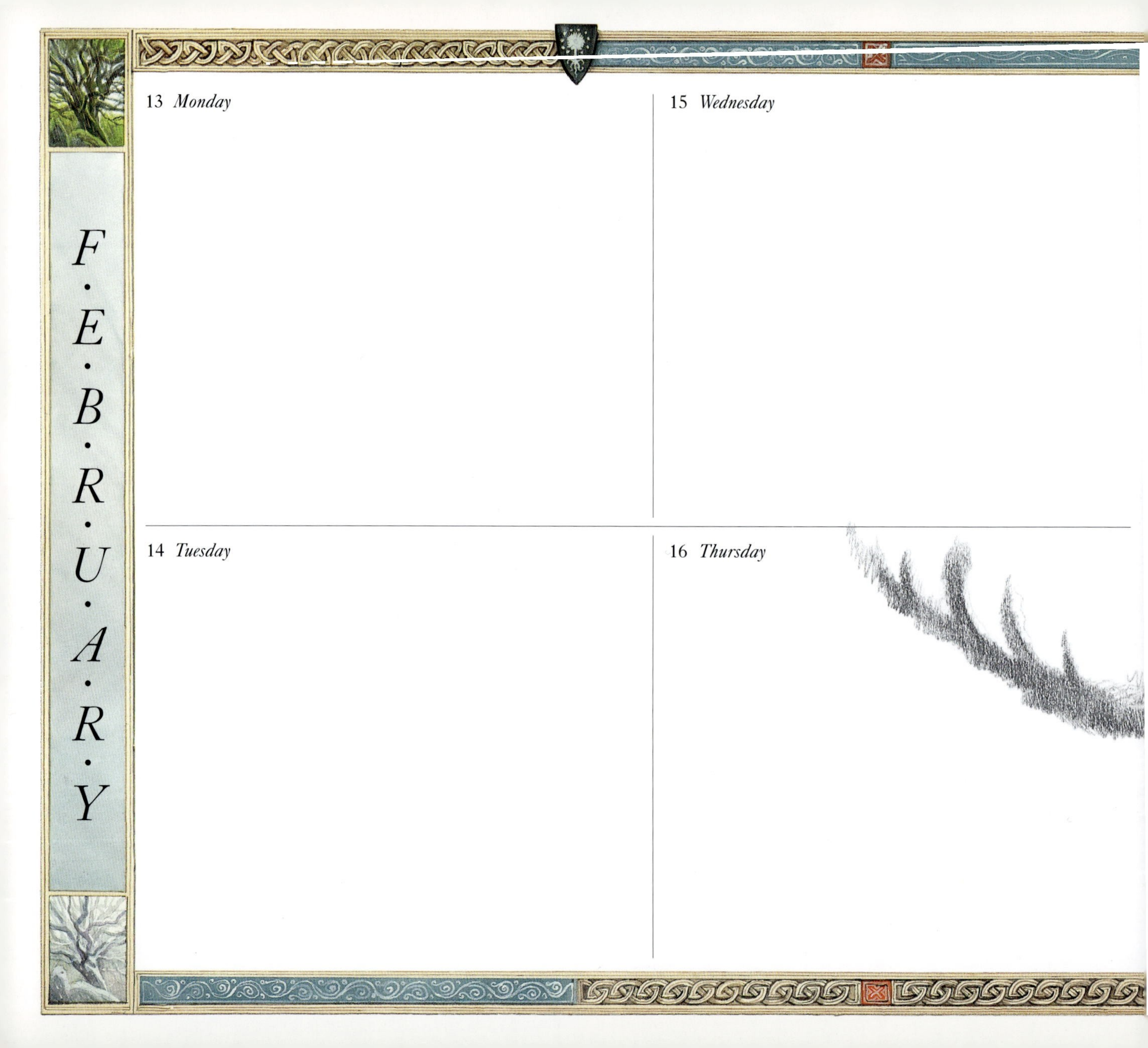

F·E·B·R·U·A·R·Y

13 *Monday*

15 *Wednesday*

14 *Tuesday*

16 *Thursday*

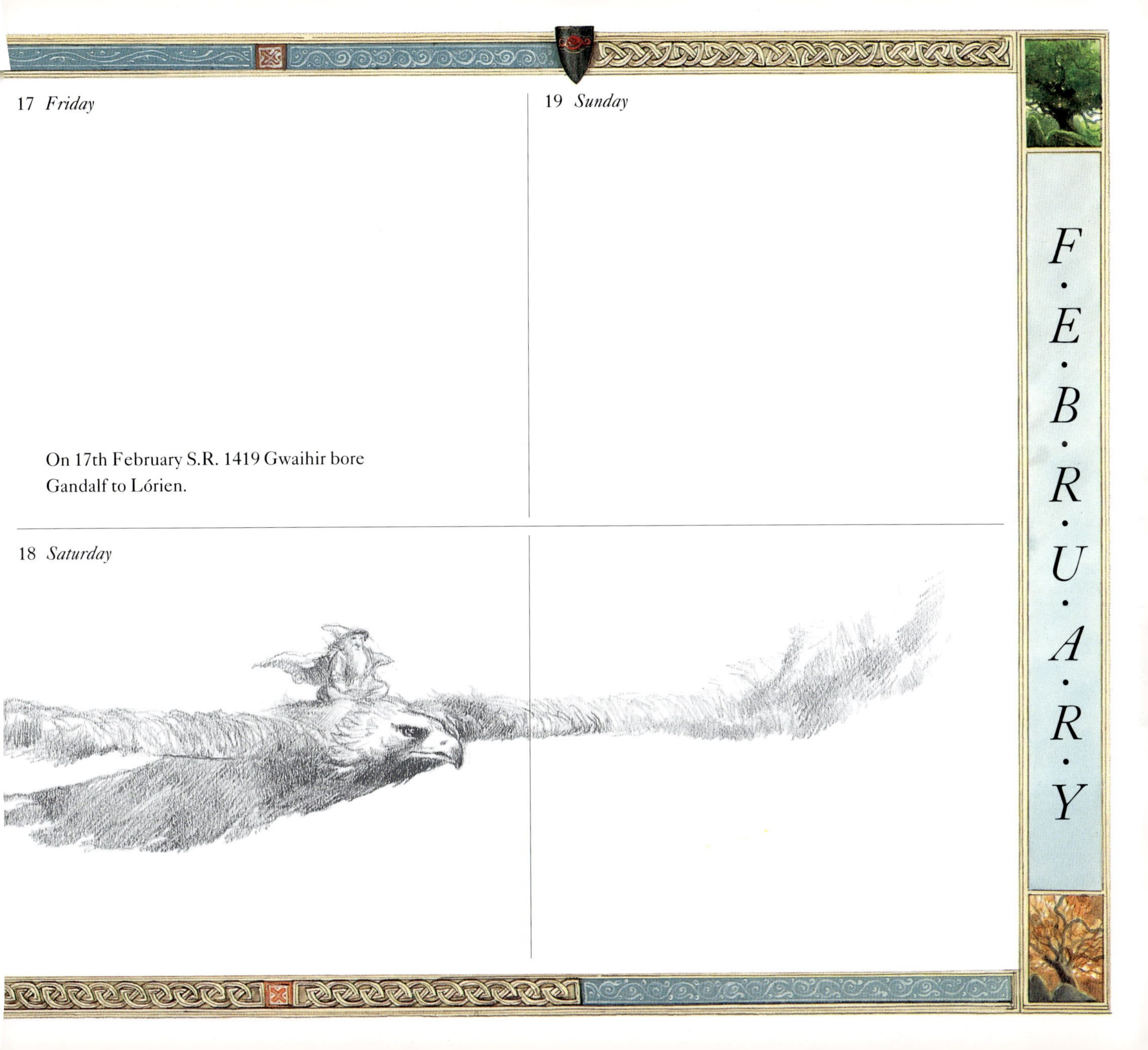

17 *Friday*

On 17th February S.R. 1419 Gwaihir bore Gandalf to Lórien.

18 *Saturday*

19 *Sunday*

F·E·B·R·U·A·R·Y

F·E·B·R·U·A·R·Y

20 *Monday*

22 *Wednesday*

21 *Tuesday*

23 *Thursday*

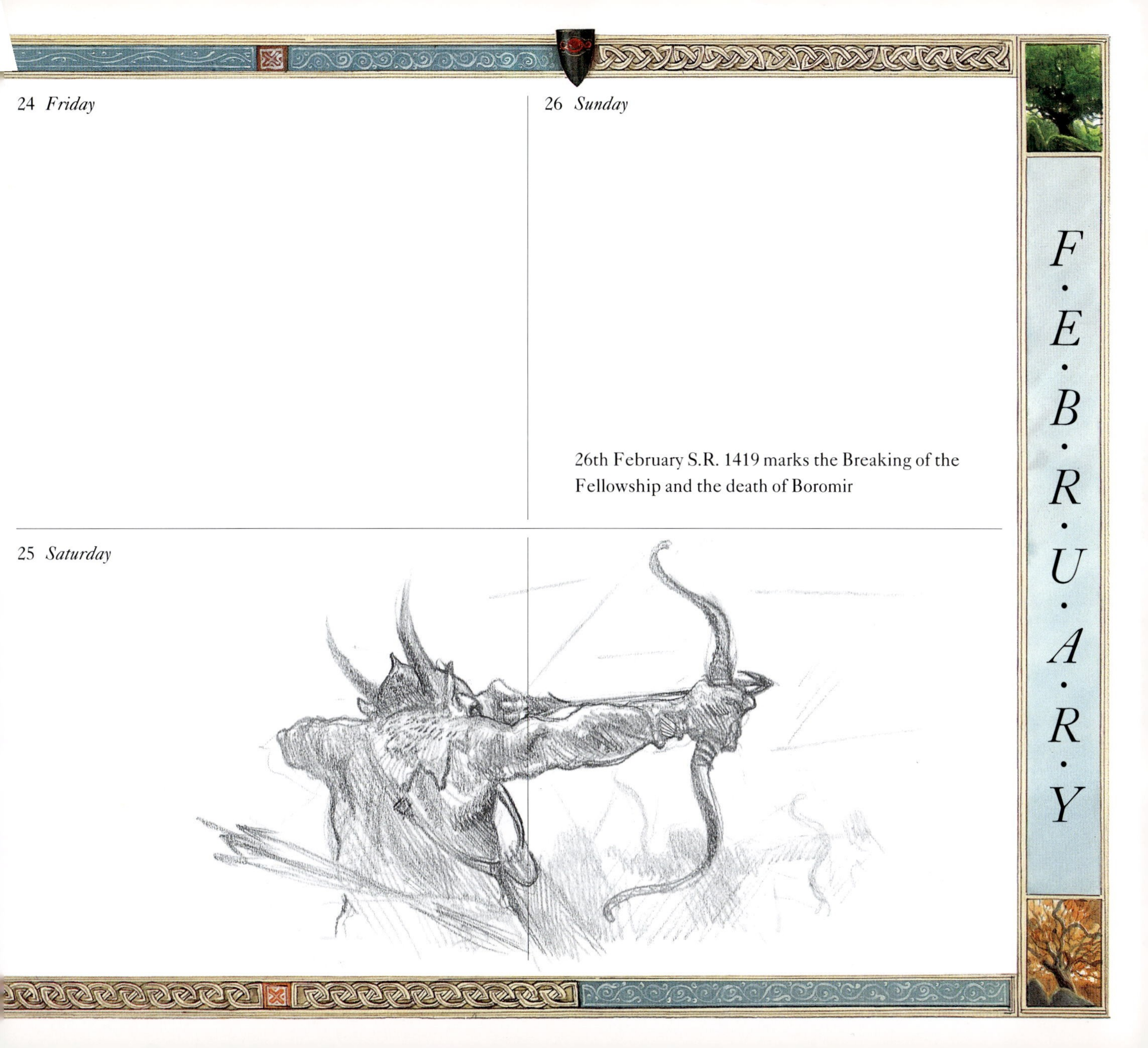

24 *Friday*

26 *Sunday*

26th February S.R. 1419 marks the Breaking of the Fellowship and the death of Boromir

25 *Saturday*

F·E·B·R·U·A·R·Y

M·A·R·C·H

27 *Monday*

1 *Wednesday*

28 *Tuesday*

2 *Thursday*

'Sam did not wait to wonder what was to be done, or whether he was brave, or loyal, or filled with rage. He sprang forward with a yell, and seized his master's sword in his left hand. Then he charged.'

THE TWO TOWERS

M·A·R·C·H

3 *Friday*

5 *Sunday*

4 *Saturday*

M·A·R·C·H
6 Monday
8 Wednesday
7 Tuesday
9 Thursday

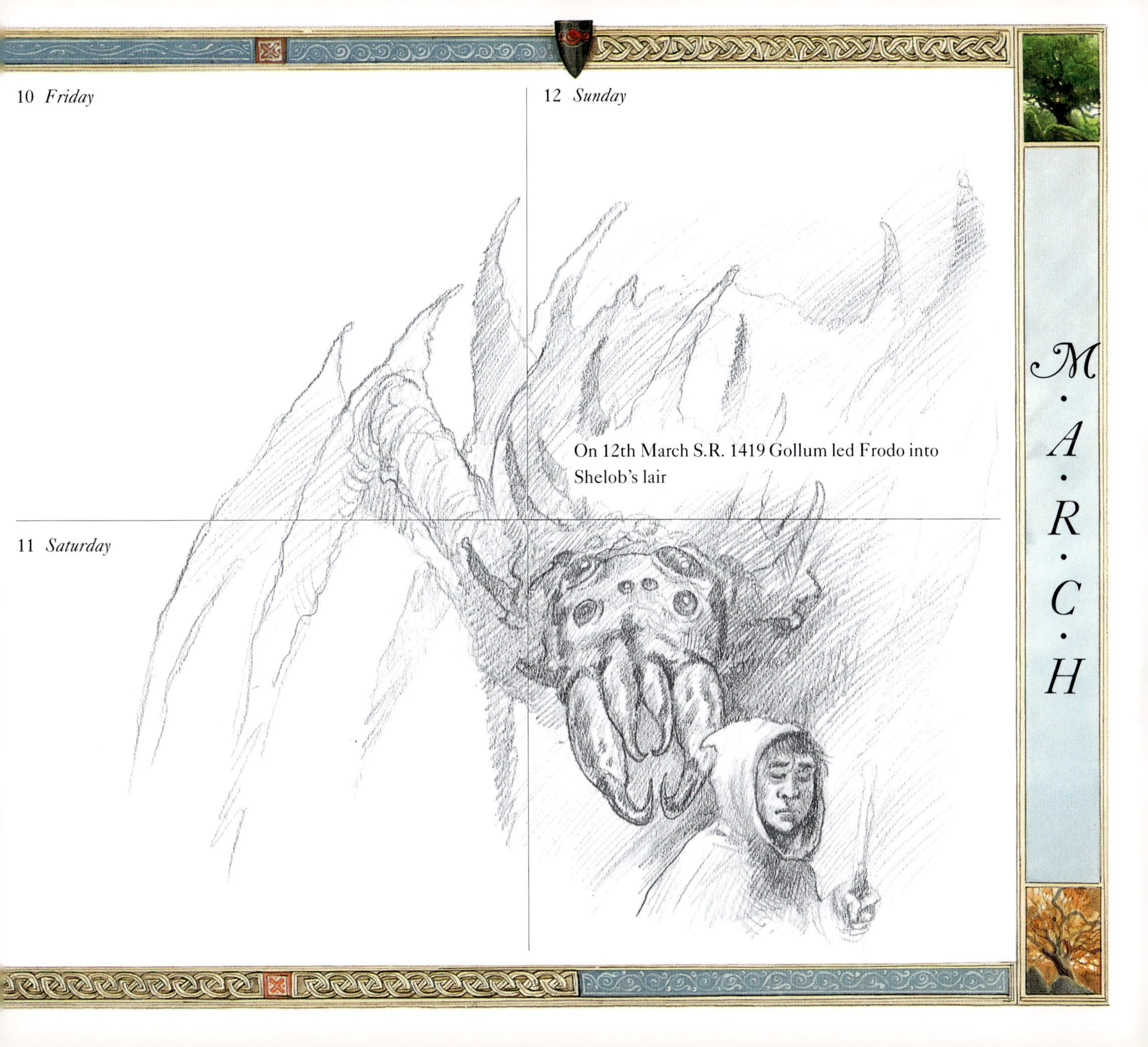

10 *Friday*

11 *Saturday*

12 *Sunday*

On 12th March S.R. 1419 Gollum led Frodo into Shelob's lair

M·A·R·C·H

M · A · R · C · H

13 *Monday*

On 13th March S.R. 1419 Frodo was captured by the Orcs of Cirith Ungol

14 *Tuesday*

15 *Wednesday*

16 *Thursday*

17 *Friday*

19 *Sunday*

18 *Saturday*

M·A·R·C·H

M·A·R·C·H

20 *Monday*

21 *Tuesday*

22 *Wednesday*

On 22nd March 1916 Ronald Tolkien and Edith Bratt were married at the Church of St Mary Immaculate in Warwick.

23 *Thursday*

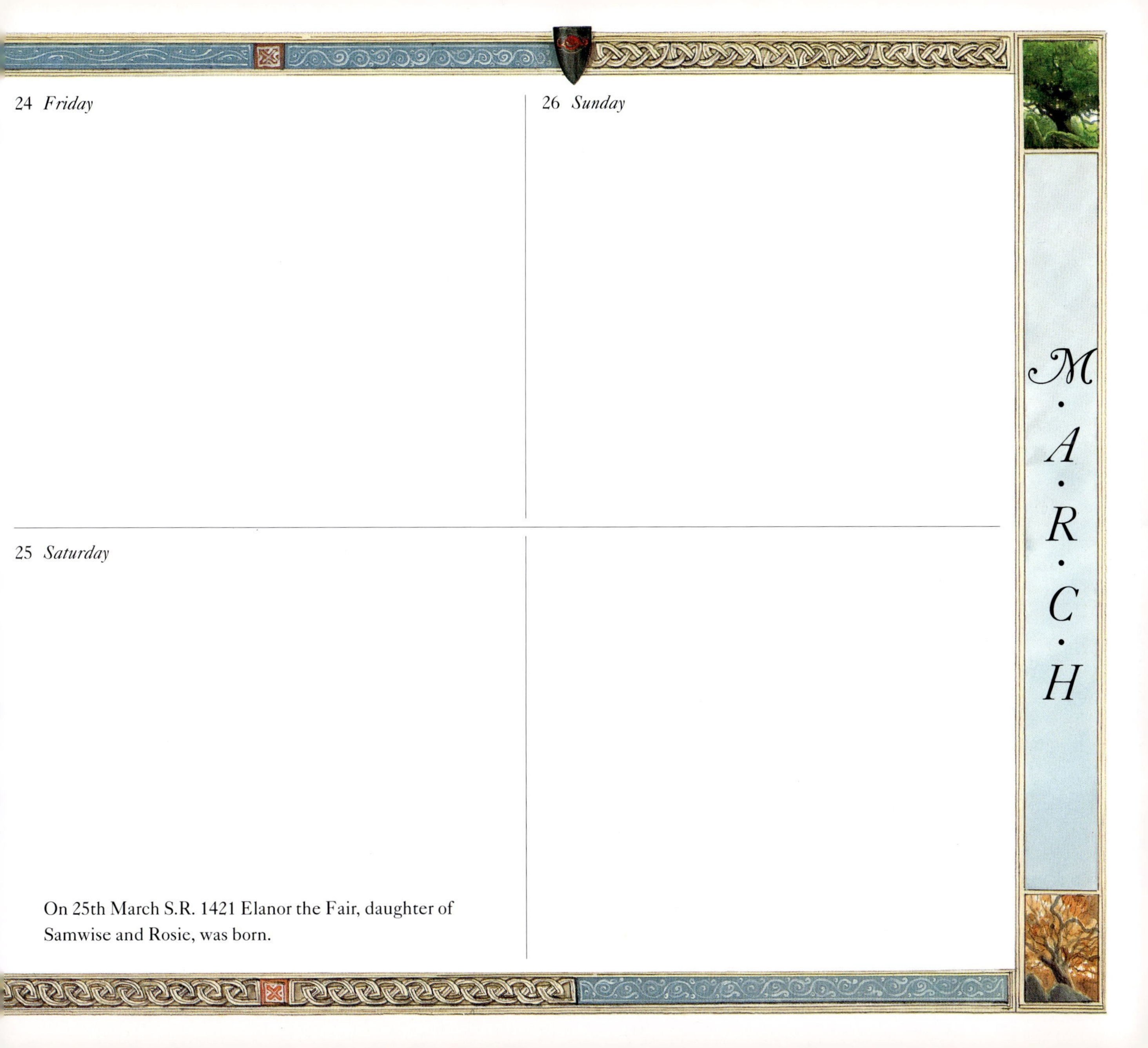

24 *Friday*

26 *Sunday*

25 *Saturday*

On 25th March S.R. 1421 Elanor the Fair, daughter of Samwise and Rosie, was born.

MARCH

27 *Monday*

28 *Tuesday*

29 *Wednesday*

30 *Thursday*

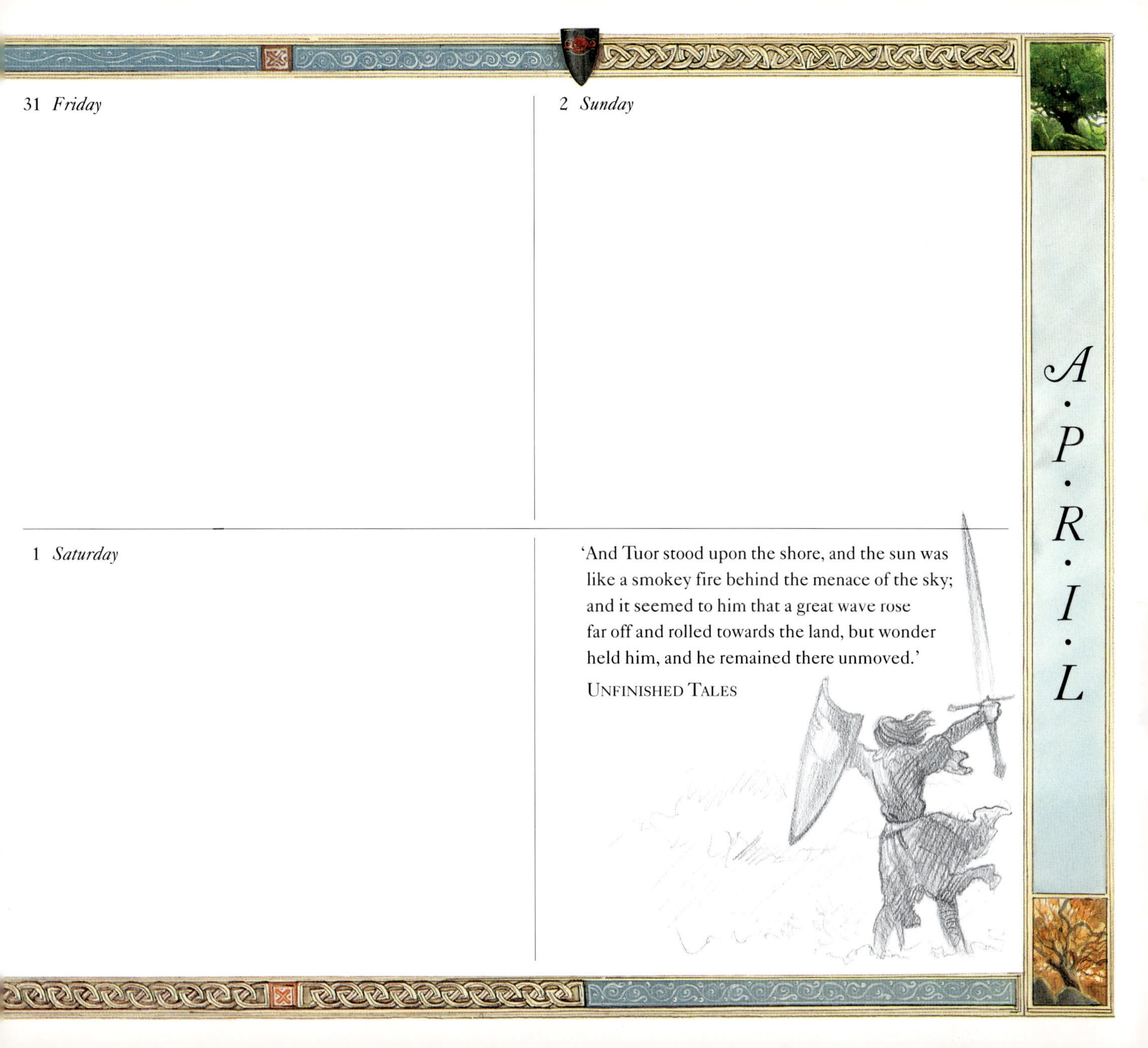

31 *Friday*

2 *Sunday*

1 *Saturday*

‘And Tuor stood upon the shore, and the sun was like a smokey fire behind the menace of the sky; and it seemed to him that a great wave rose far off and rolled towards the land, but wonder held him, and he remained there unmoved.’

UNFINISHED TALES

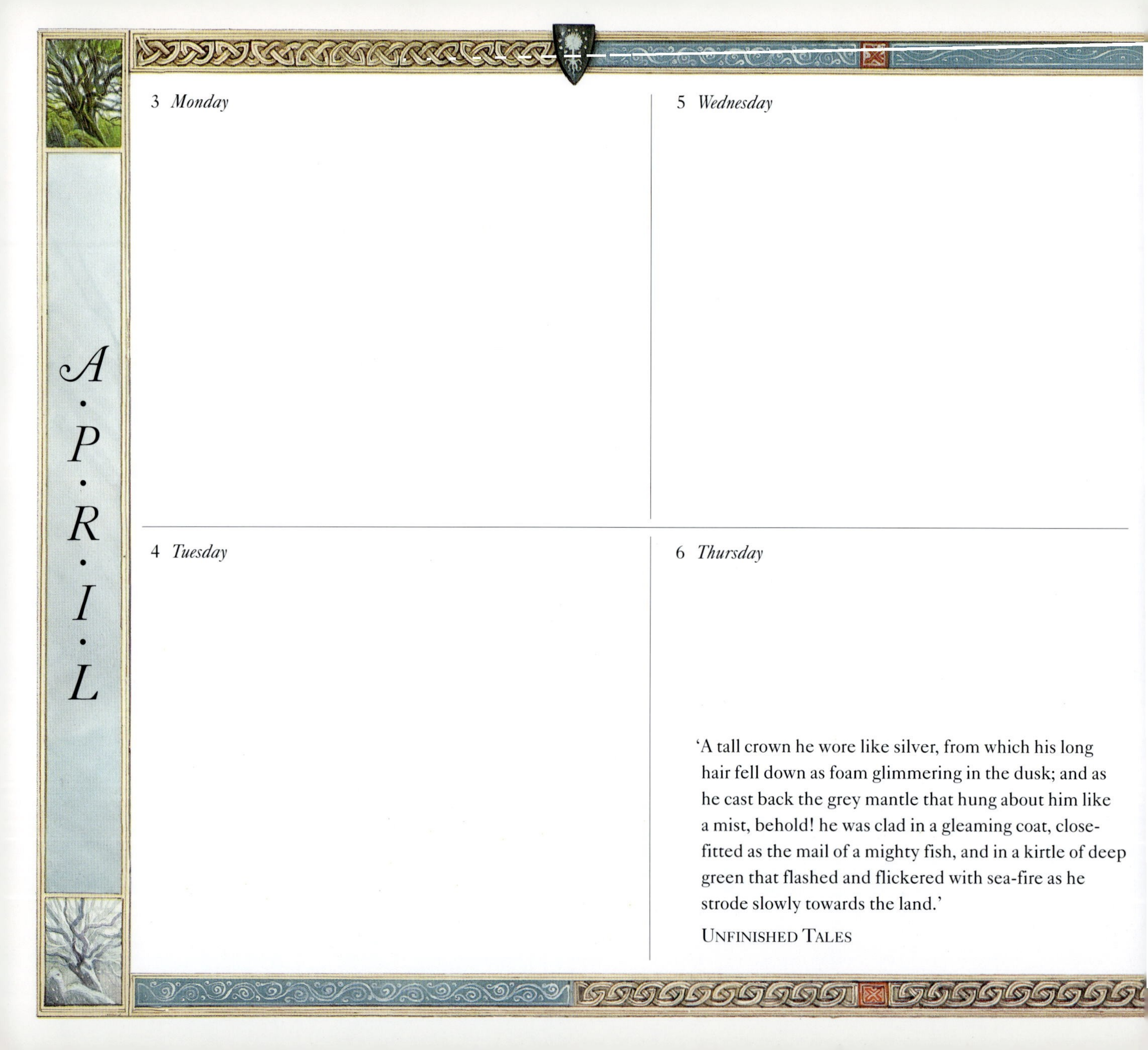

A·P·R·I·L

3 *Monday*

4 *Tuesday*

5 *Wednesday*

6 *Thursday*

'A tall crown he wore like silver, from which his long hair fell down as foam glimmering in the dusk; and as he cast back the grey mantle that hung about him like a mist, behold! he was clad in a gleaming coat, close-fitted as the mail of a mighty fish, and in a kirtle of deep green that flashed and flickered with sea-fire as he strode slowly towards the land.'

UNFINISHED TALES

A·P·R·I·L

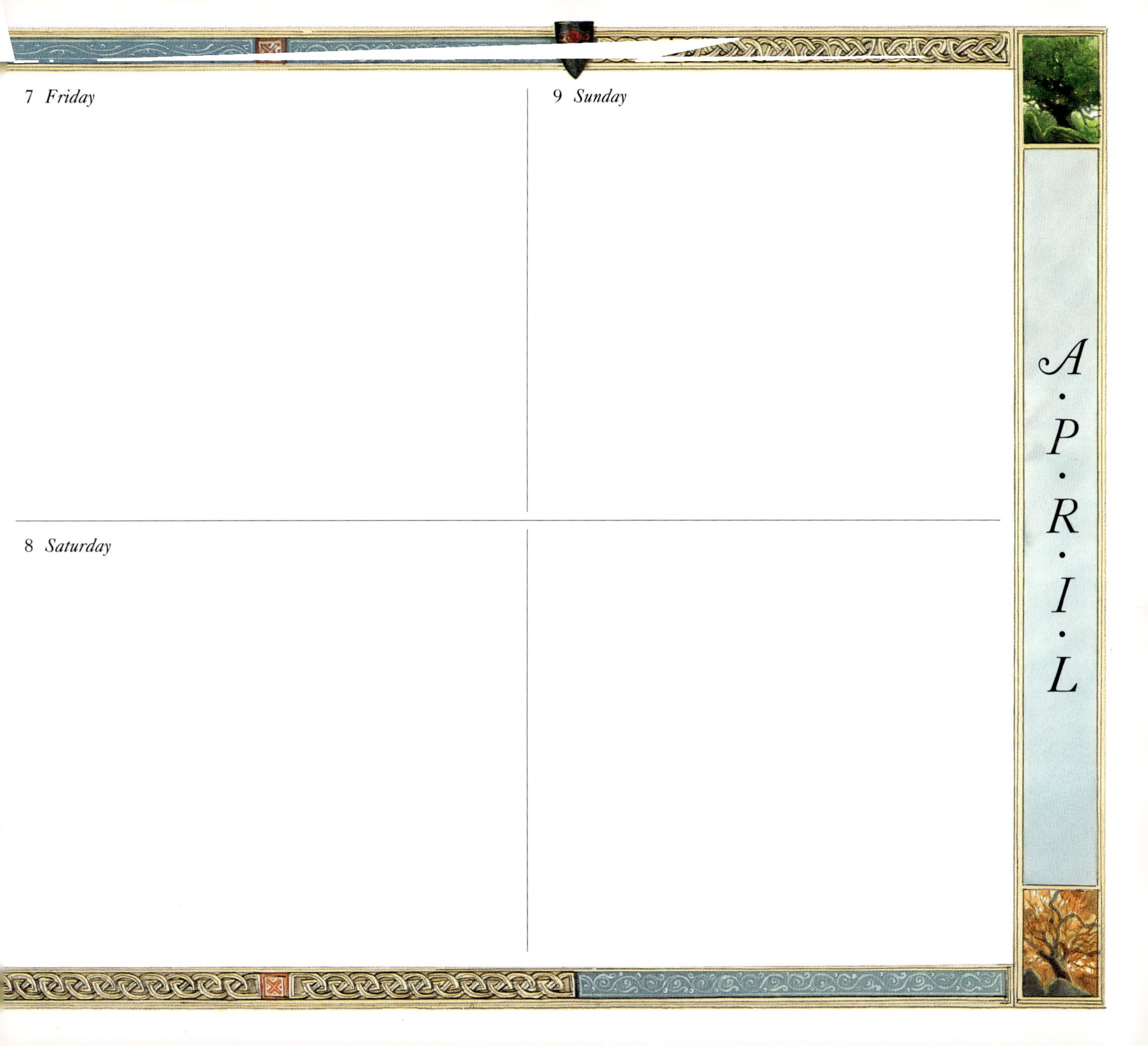

7 *Friday*

9 *Sunday*

8 *Saturday*

A·P·R·I·L

10 *Monday*

11 *Tuesday*

12 *Wednesday*

13 *Thursday*

14 *Friday*

16 *Sunday*

15 *Saturday*

'In the Party Field a beautiful young sapling leaped up: it had silver bark and long leaves and burst into golden flowers in April.'

THE RETURN OF THE KING

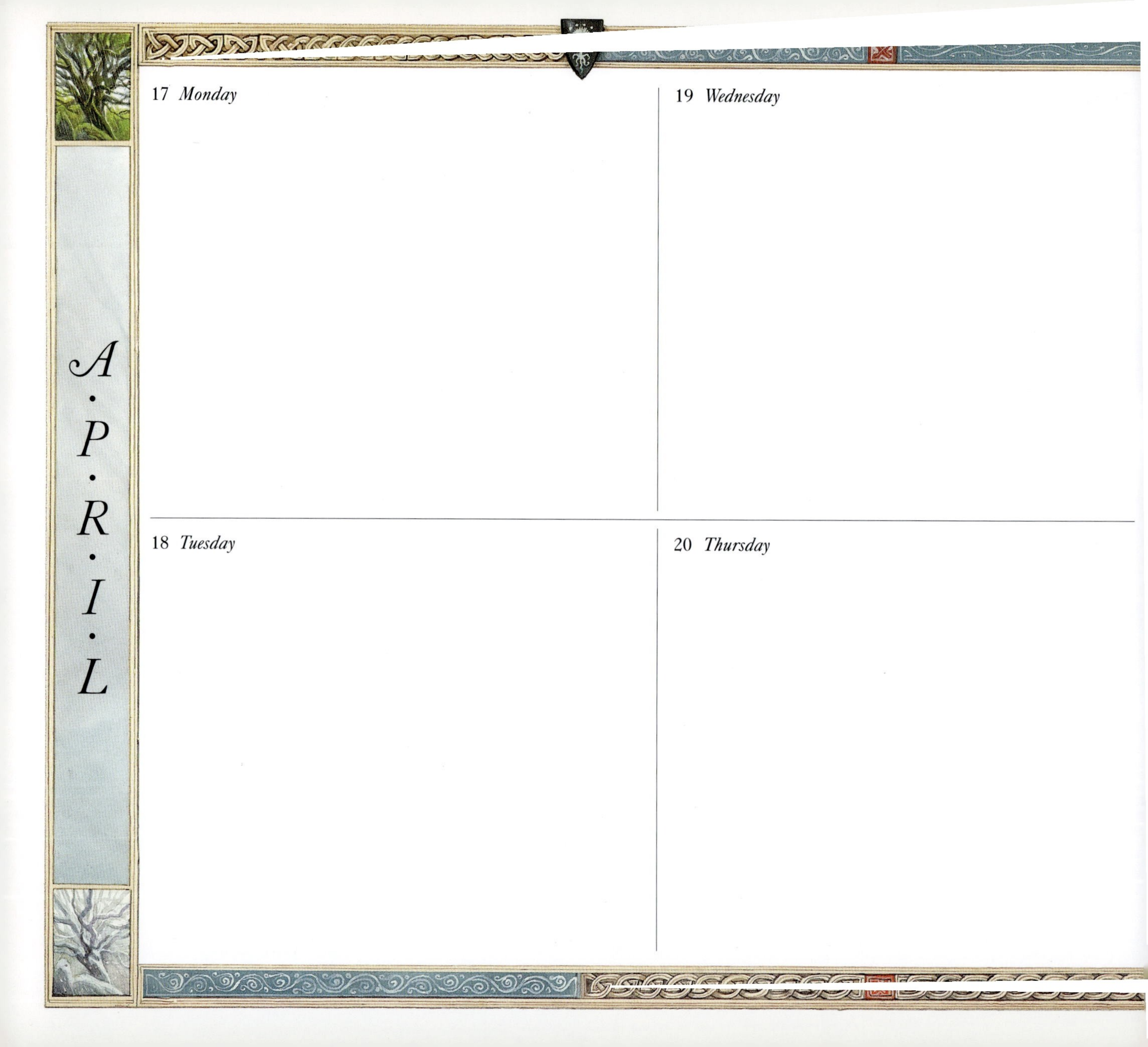

17 *Monday*

18 *Tuesday*

19 *Wednesday*

20 *Thursday*

21 *Friday*

23 *Sunday*

22 *Saturday*

A·P·R·I·L

A·P·R·I·L

24 *Monday*

25 *Tuesday*

26 *Wednesday*

27 *Thursday*

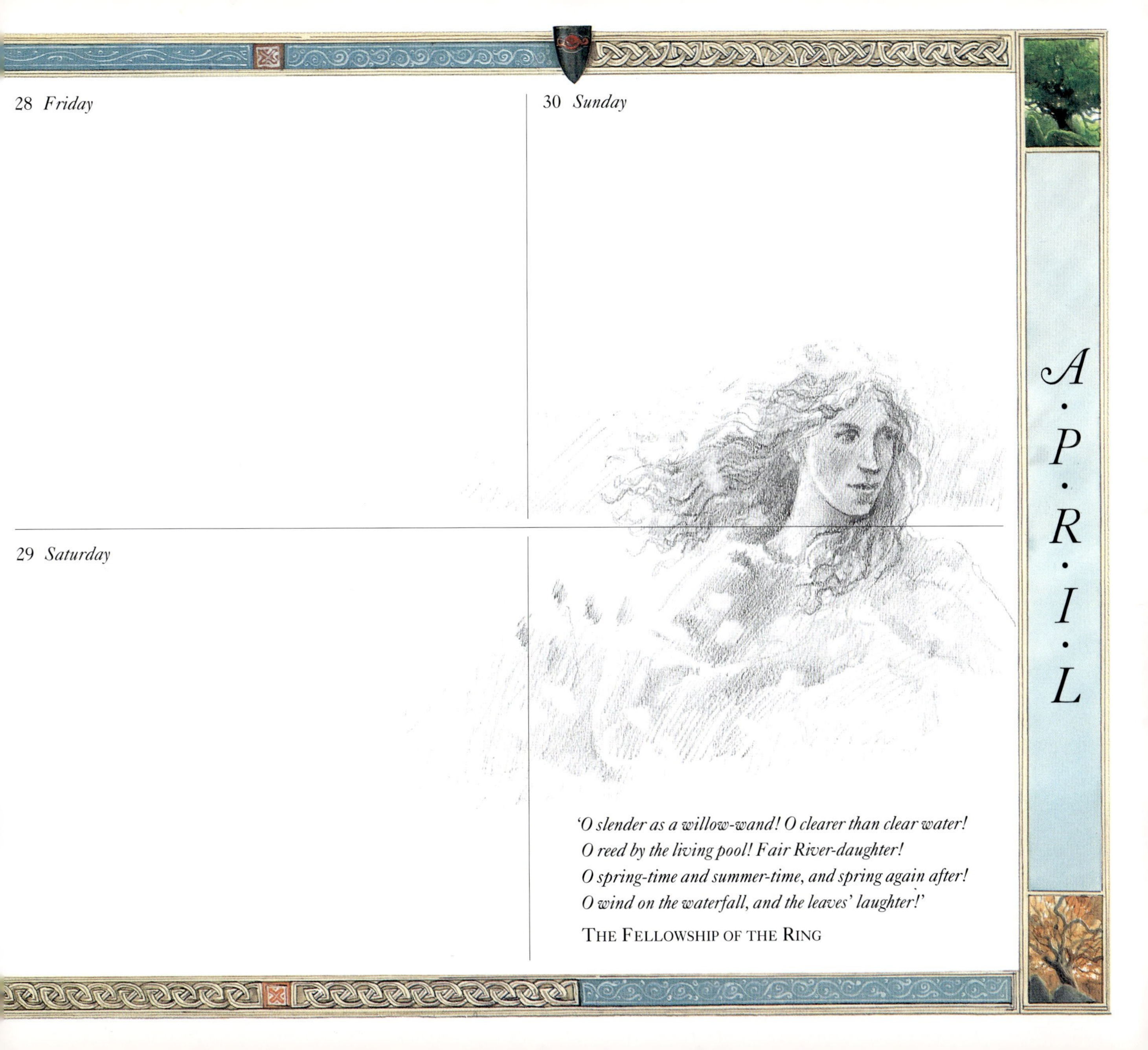

28 *Friday*

29 *Saturday*

30 *Sunday*

'O slender as a willow-wand! O clearer than clear water!
O reed by the living pool! Fair River-daughter!
O spring-time and summer-time, and spring again after!
O wind on the waterfall, and the leaves' laughter!'

THE FELLOWSHIP OF THE RING

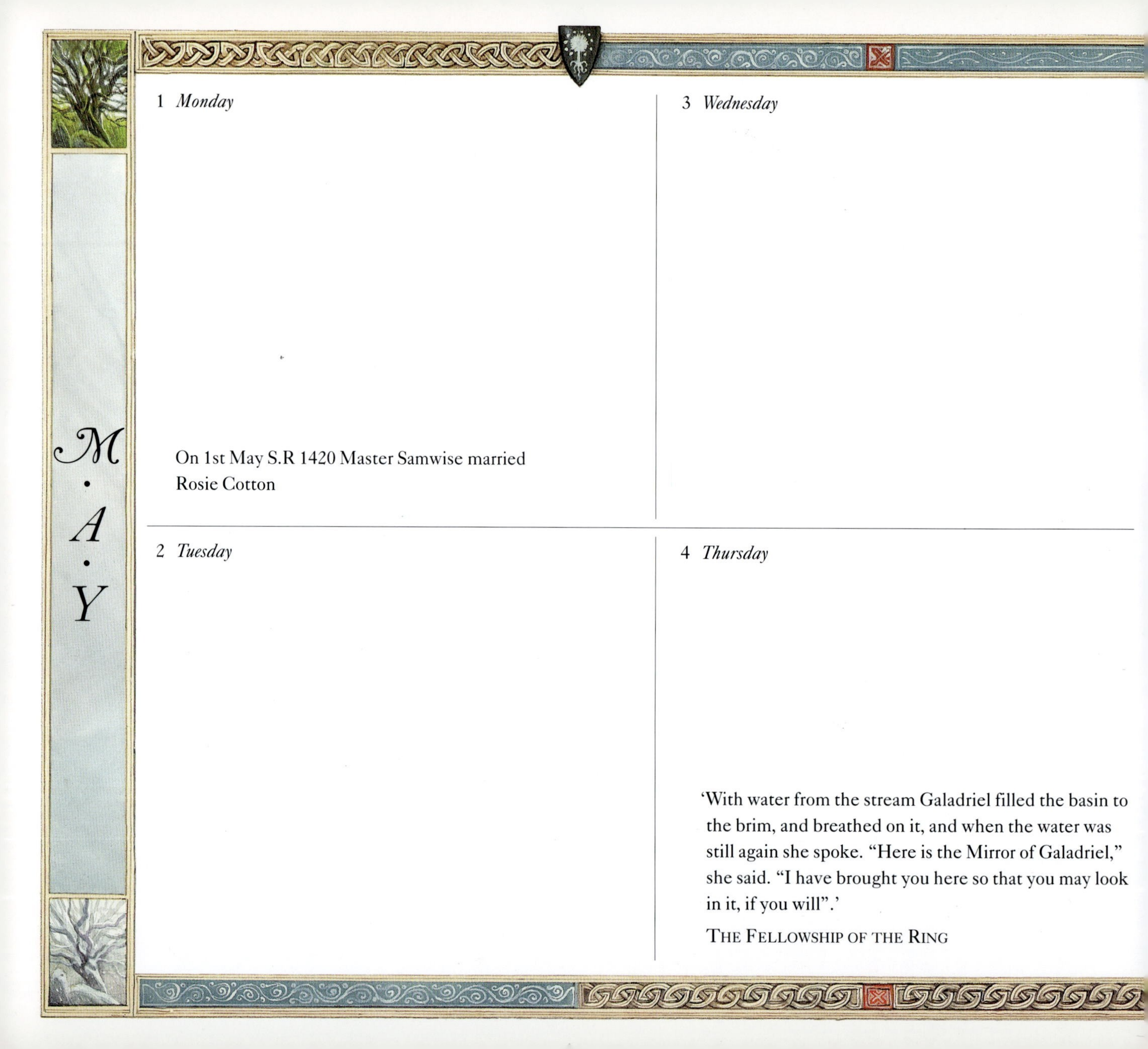

M · A · Y

1 *Monday*

On 1st May S.R 1420 Master Samwise married Rosie Cotton

2 *Tuesday*

3 *Wednesday*

4 *Thursday*

'With water from the stream Galadriel filled the basin to the brim, and breathed on it, and when the water was still again she spoke. "Here is the Mirror of Galadriel," she said. "I have brought you here so that you may look in it, if you will".'

THE FELLOWSHIP OF THE RING

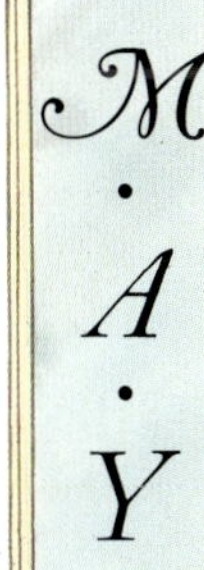
M·A·Y

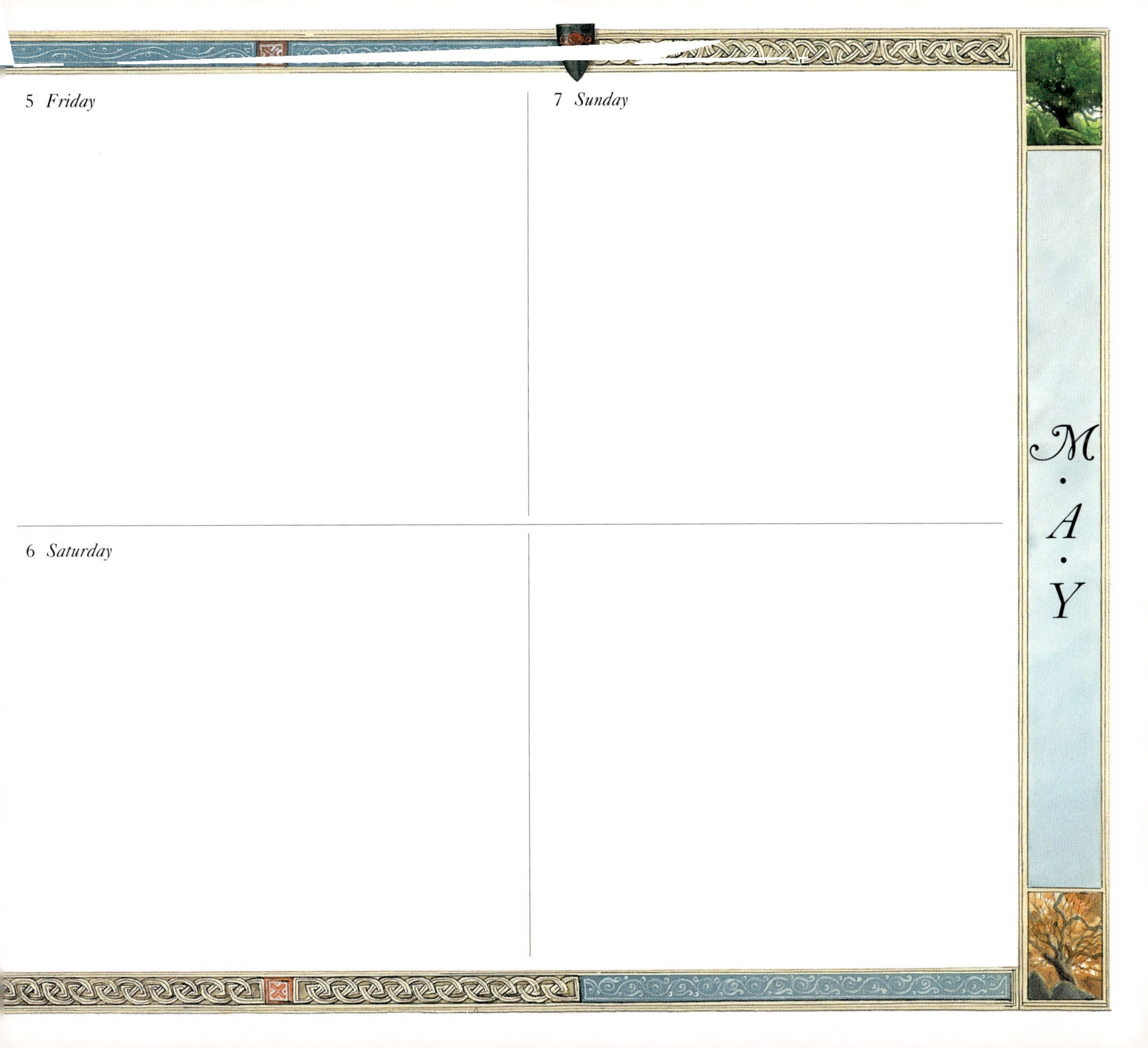

5 *Friday*

6 *Saturday*

7 *Sunday*

MAY

M · A · Y

8 *Monday*

10 *Wednesday*

9 *Tuesday*

11 *Thursday*

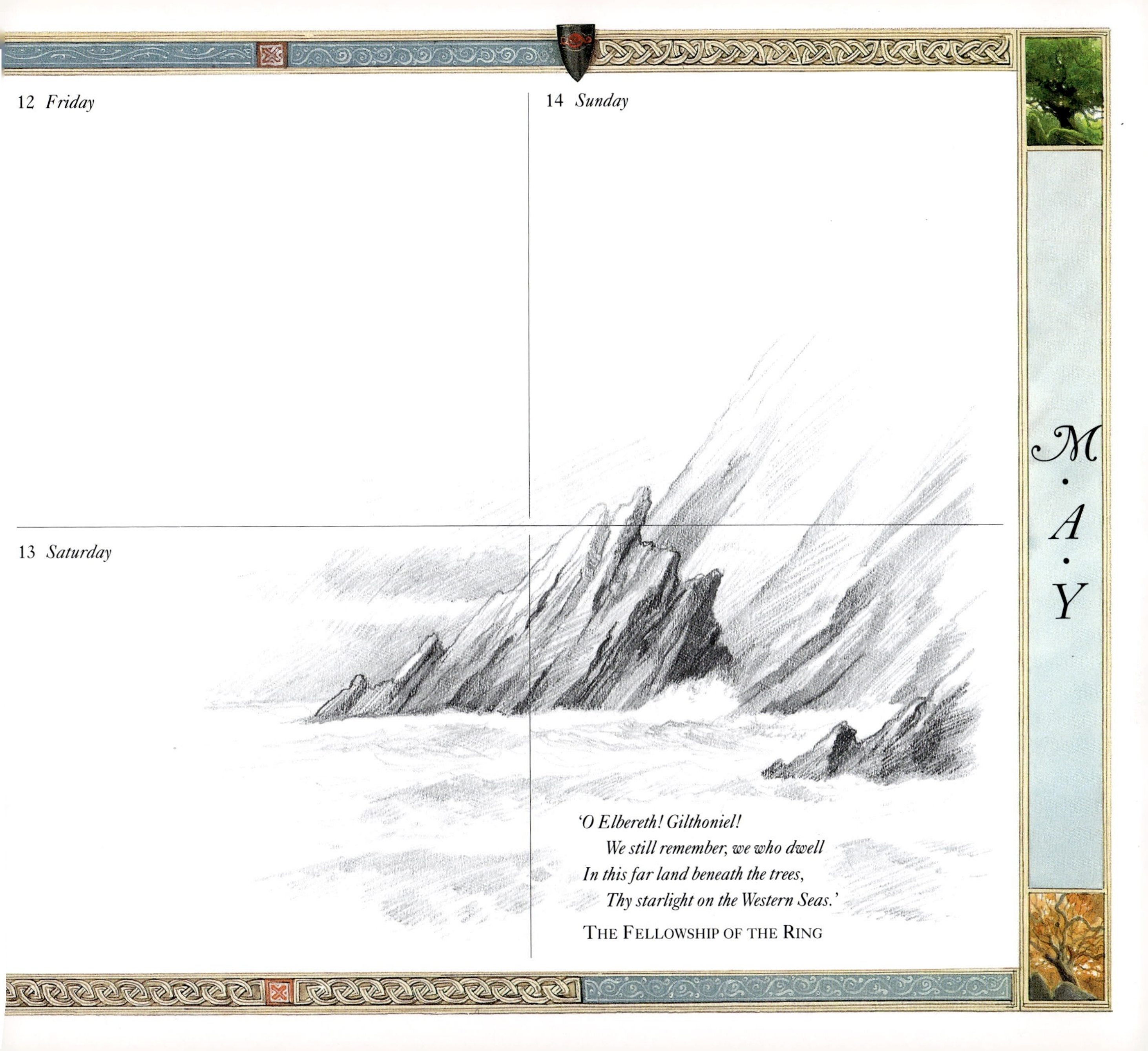

12 *Friday*

14 *Sunday*

13 *Saturday*

'O Elbereth! Gilthoniel!
We still remember, we who dwell
In this far land beneath the trees,
Thy starlight on the Western Seas.'

THE FELLOWSHIP OF THE RING

M·A·Y

M·A·Y

15 *Monday*

17 *Wednesday*

16 *Tuesday*

18 *Thursday*

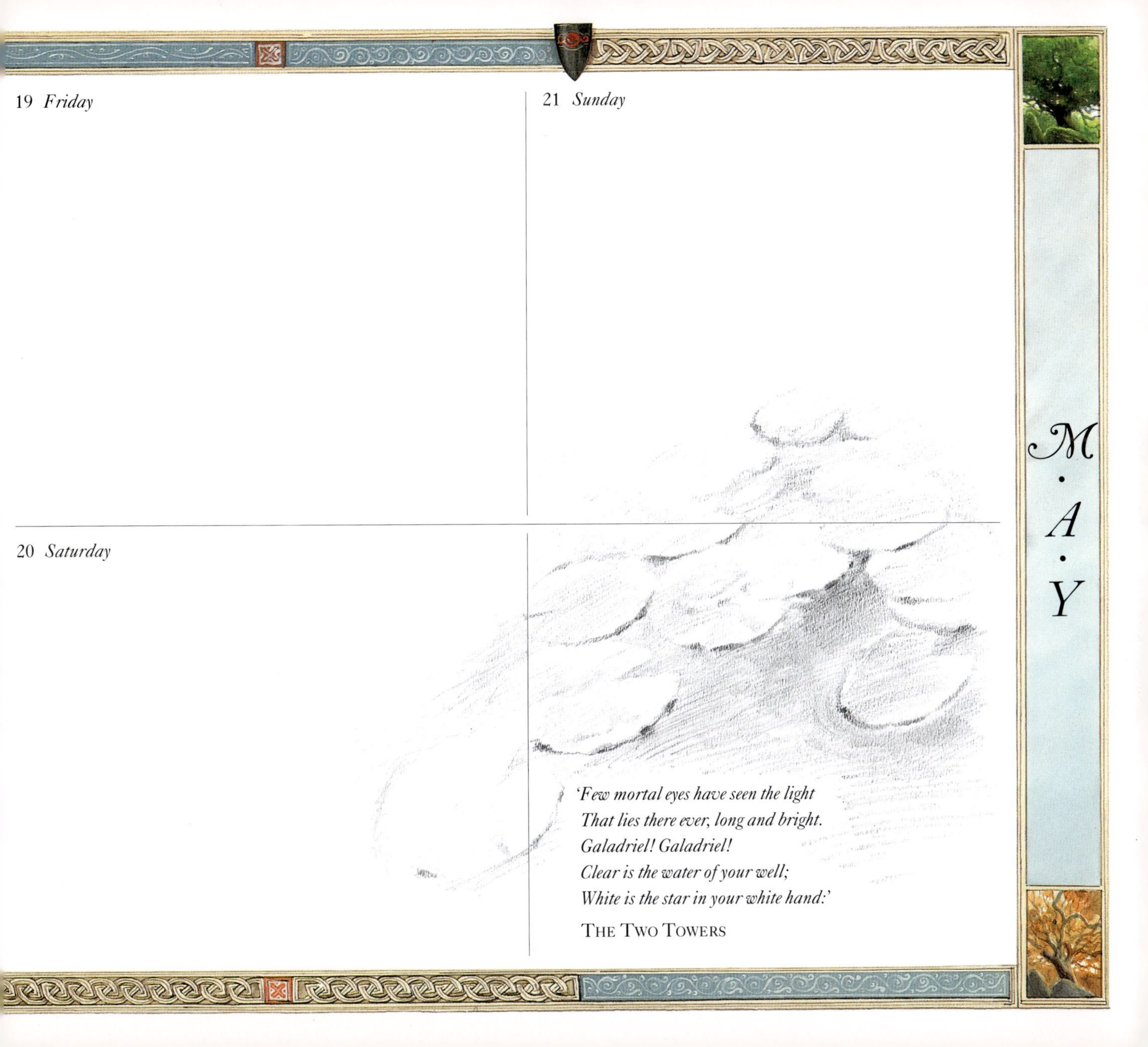

19 *Friday*

21 *Sunday*

20 *Saturday*

'Few mortal eyes have seen the light
That lies there ever, long and bright.
Galadriel! Galadriel!
Clear is the water of your well;
White is the star in your white hand:'

THE TWO TOWERS

M·A·Y

22 *Monday*

24 *Wednesday*

23 *Tuesday*

25 *Thursday*

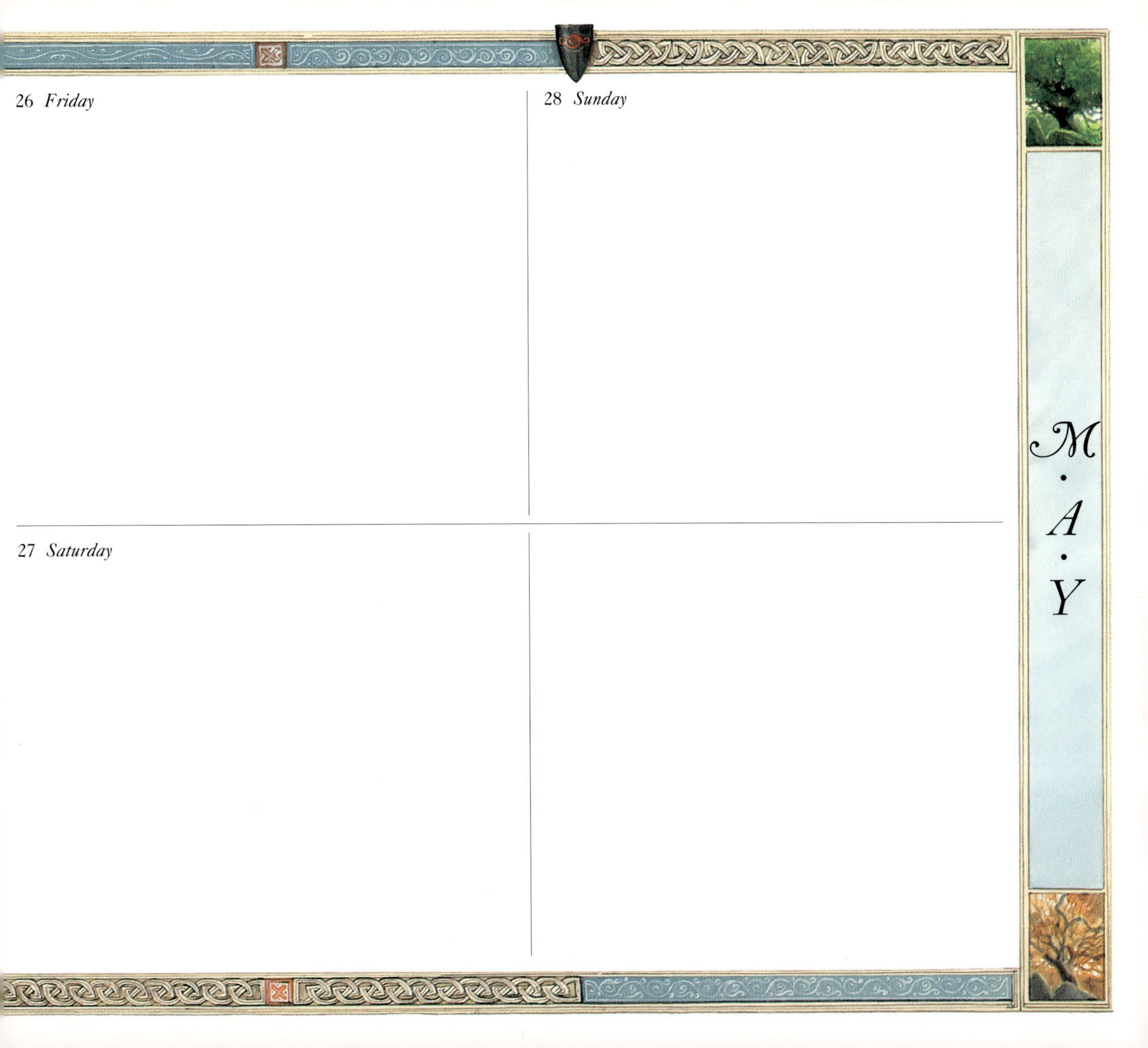

26 *Friday*

28 *Sunday*

27 *Saturday*

M · A · Y

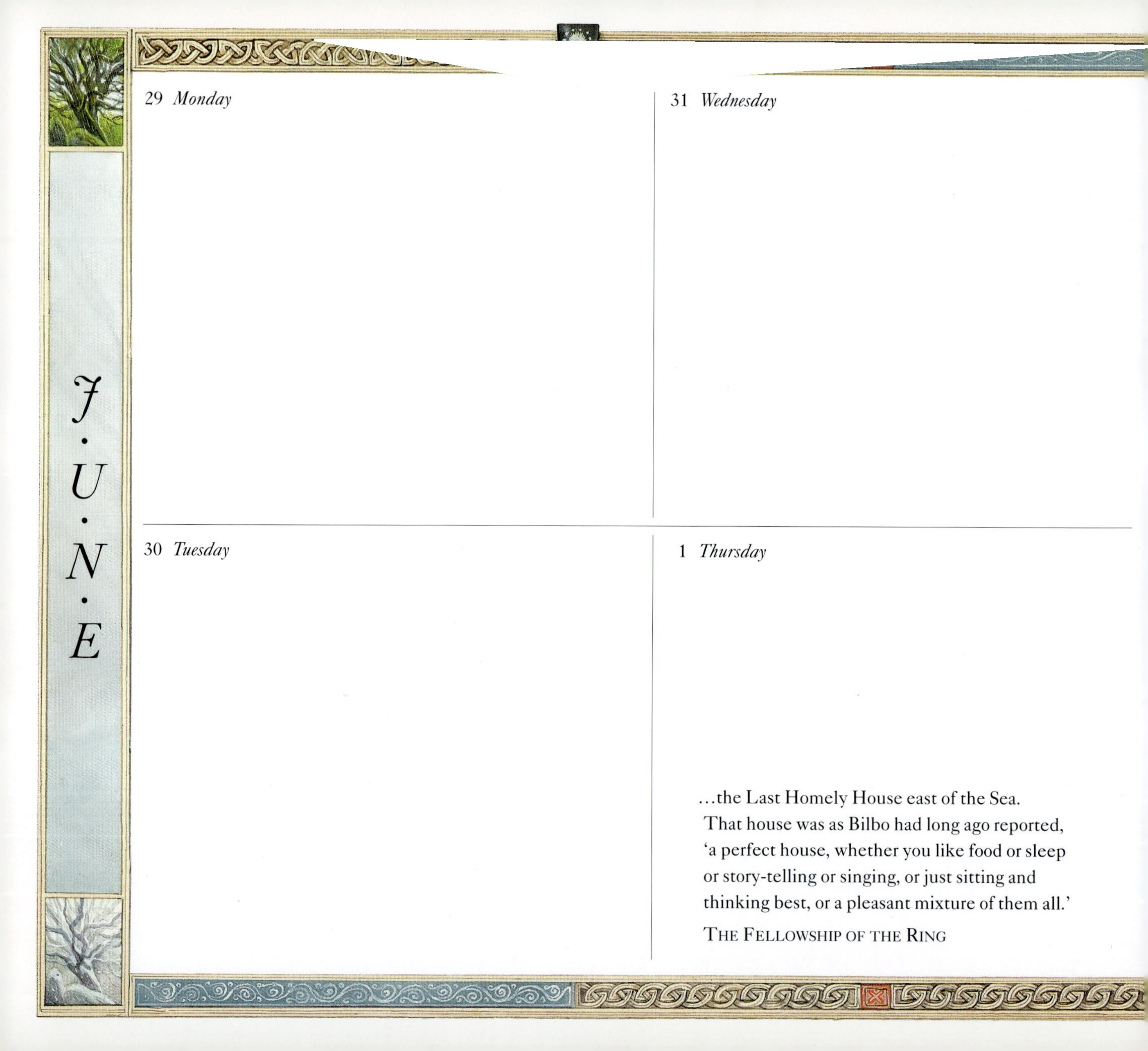

29 *Monday*

30 *Tuesday*

31 *Wednesday*

1 *Thursday*

...the Last Homely House east of the Sea. That house was as Bilbo had long ago reported, 'a perfect house, whether you like food or sleep or story-telling or singing, or just sitting and thinking best, or a pleasant mixture of them all.'

THE FELLOWSHIP OF THE RING

J·U·N·E

2 *Friday*

4 *Sunday*

On 4th June 1916, shortly after his marriage to Edith, J.R.R. Tolkien embarked for France with the Lancashire Fusiliers, bound for the Somme.

3 *Saturday*

J·U·N·E

5 *Monday*

6 *Tuesday*

7 *Wednesday*

8 *Thursday*

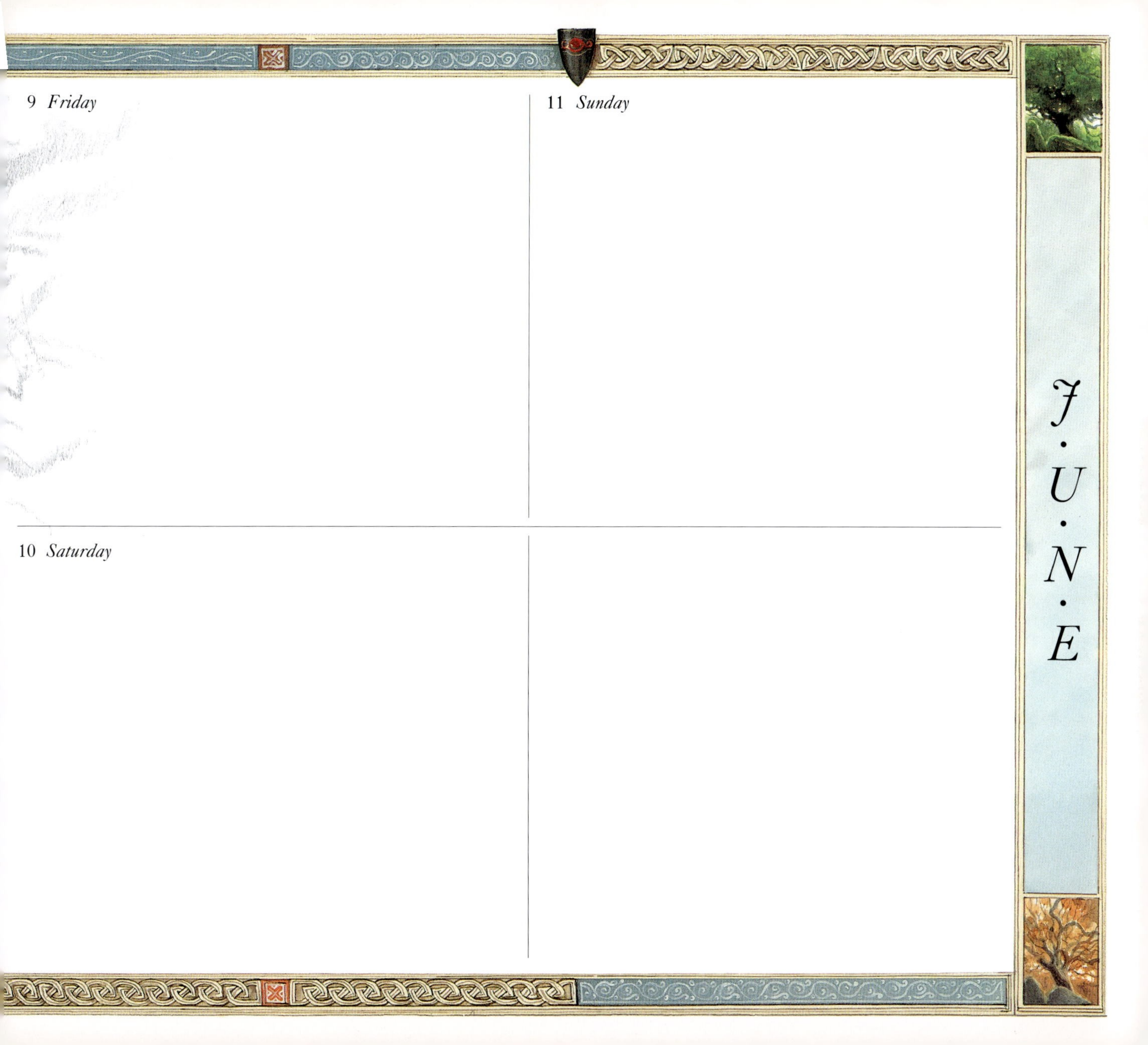

9 *Friday*

11 *Sunday*

10 *Saturday*

12 *Monday*

13 *Tuesday*

14 *Wednesday*

On 14th June S.R. 1419 the sons of Elrond met Arwen's escort and brought her to Edoras.

15 *Thursday*

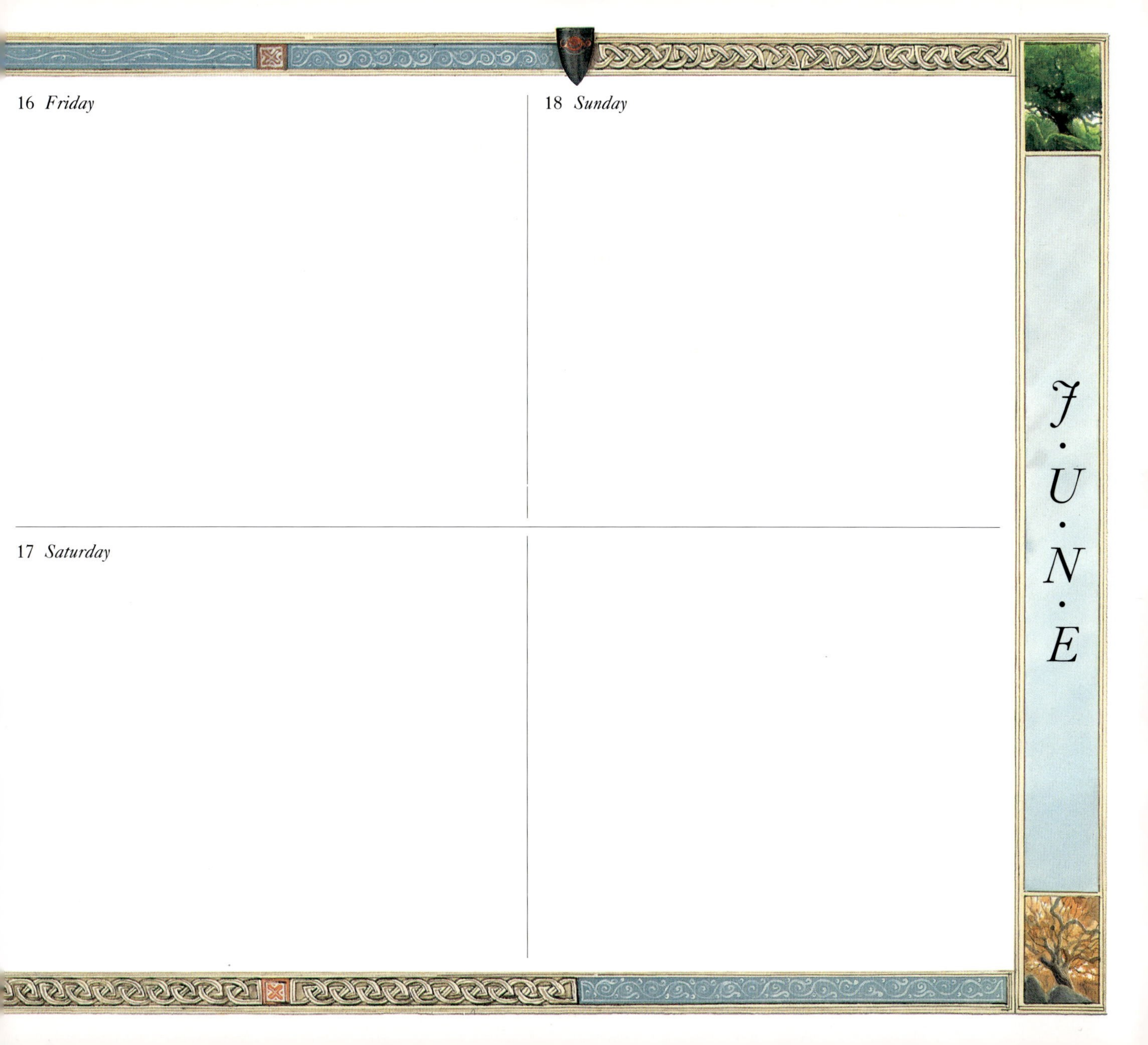

16 *Friday*

18 *Sunday*

17 *Saturday*

J · U · N · E

J·U·N·E

19 *Monday*

21 *Wednesday*

20 *Tuesday*

22 *Thursday*

On 20th June S.R. 1418 Sauron attacked Osgiliath.

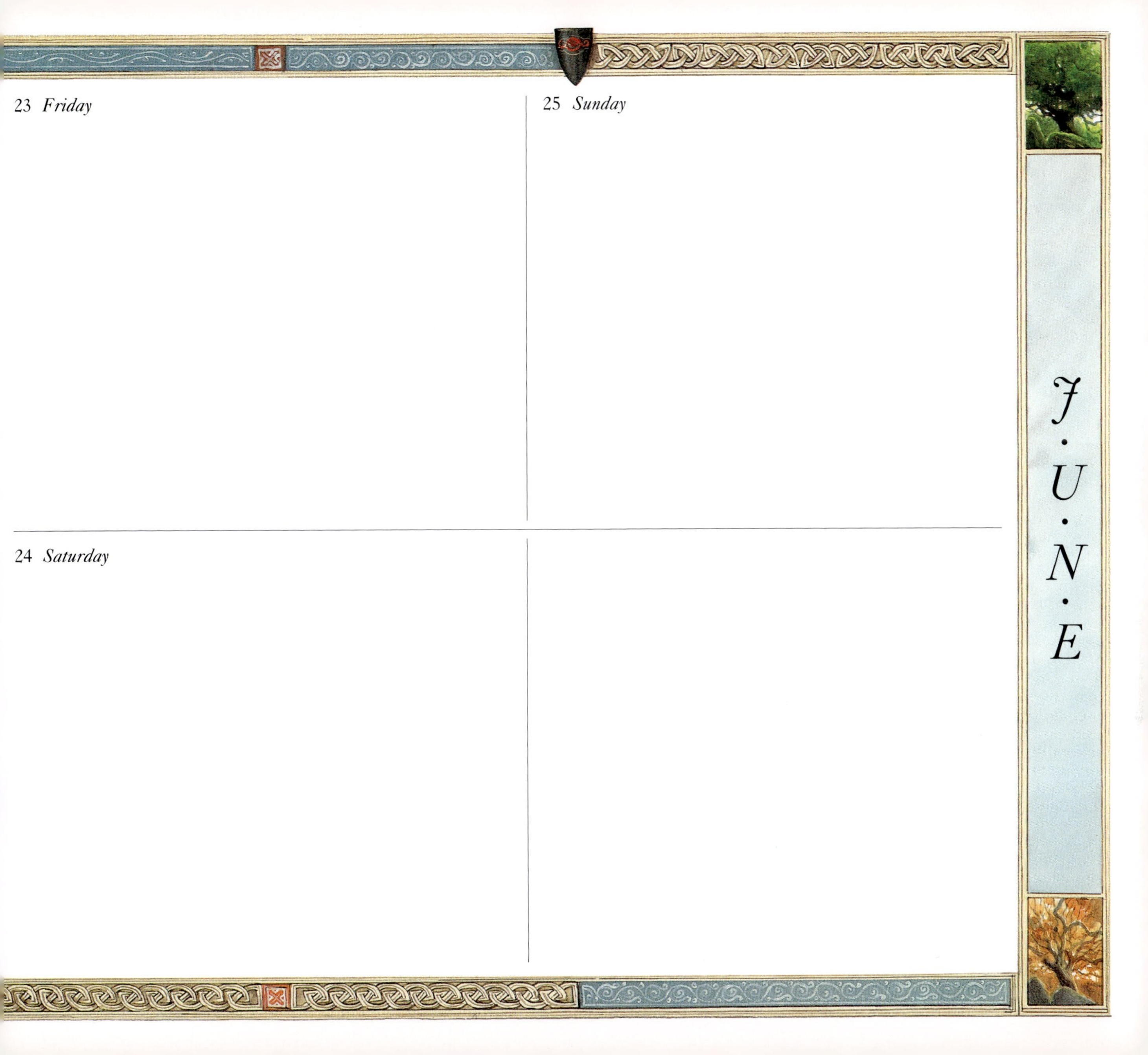

23 *Friday*

25 *Sunday*

24 *Saturday*

J·U·N·E

26 *Monday*

27 *Tuesday*

28 *Wednesday*

29 *Thursday*

30 *Friday*

1 *Saturday*

2 *Sunday*

J·U·L·Y

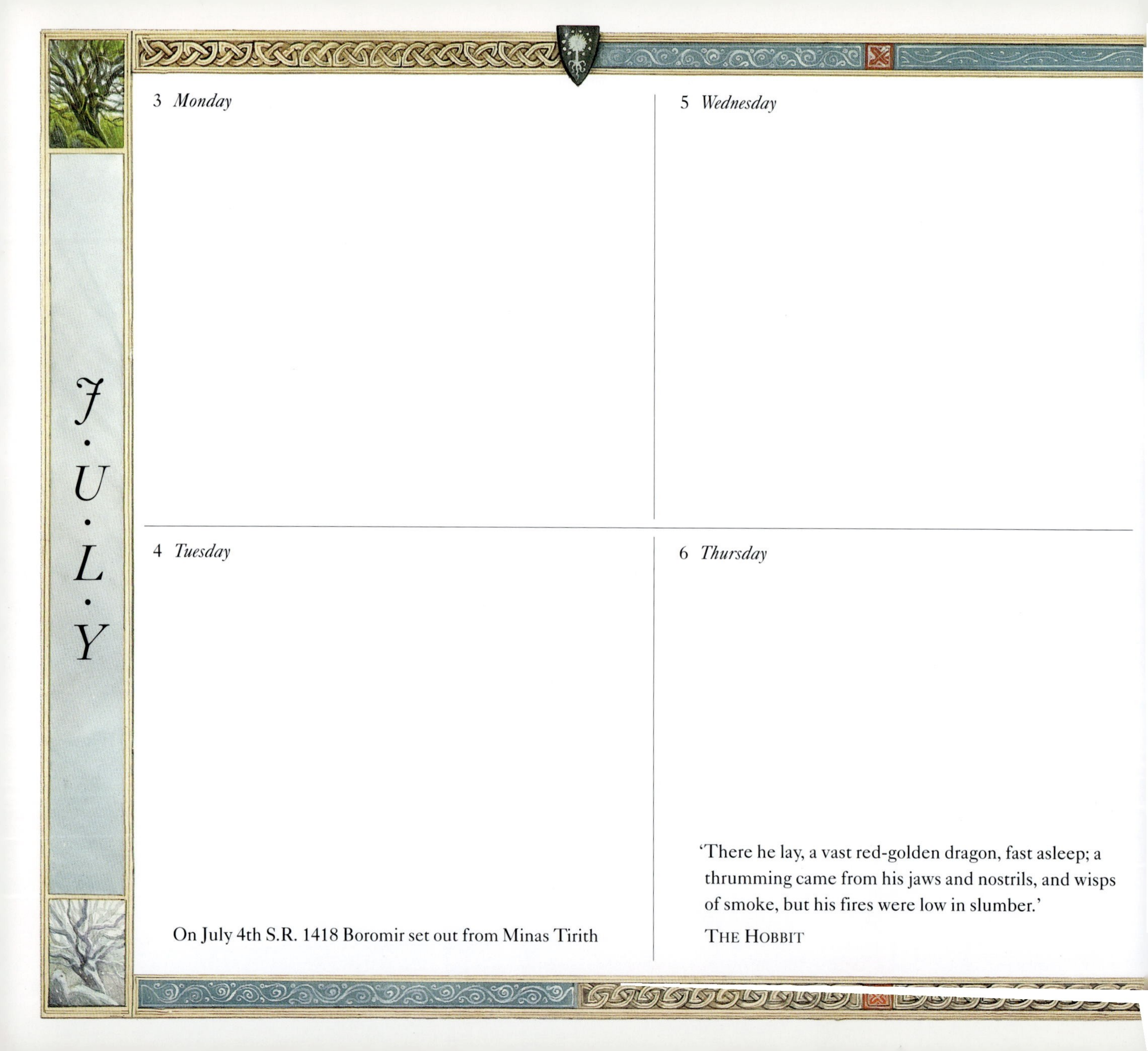

J·U·L·Y

3 *Monday*

4 *Tuesday*

On July 4th S.R. 1418 Boromir set out from Minas Tirith

5 *Wednesday*

6 *Thursday*

'There he lay, a vast red-golden dragon, fast asleep; a thrumming came from his jaws and nostrils, and wisps of smoke, but his fires were low in slumber.'

THE HOBBIT

J·U·L·Y

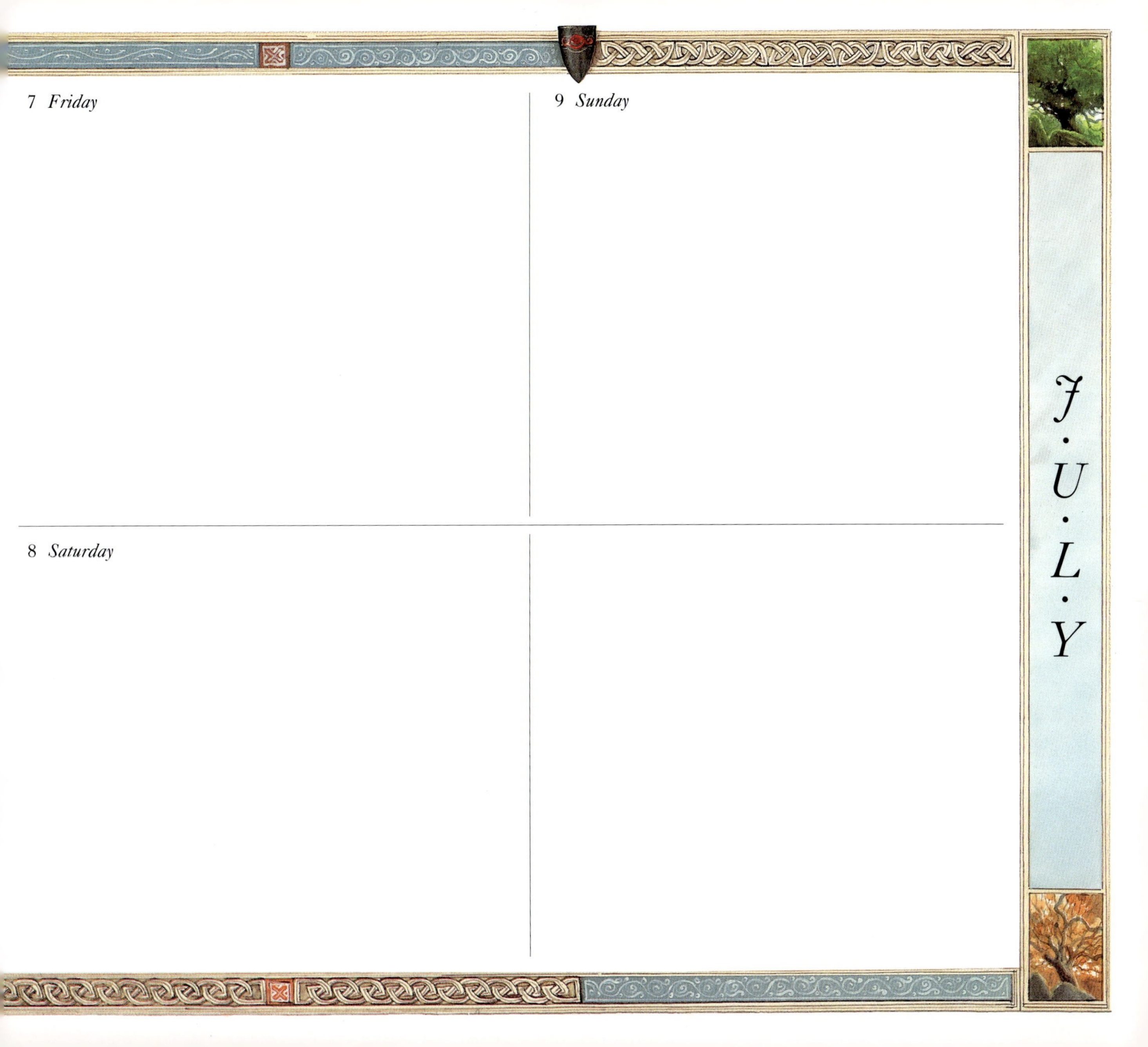

7 *Friday*

9 *Sunday*

8 *Saturday*

J·U·L·Y

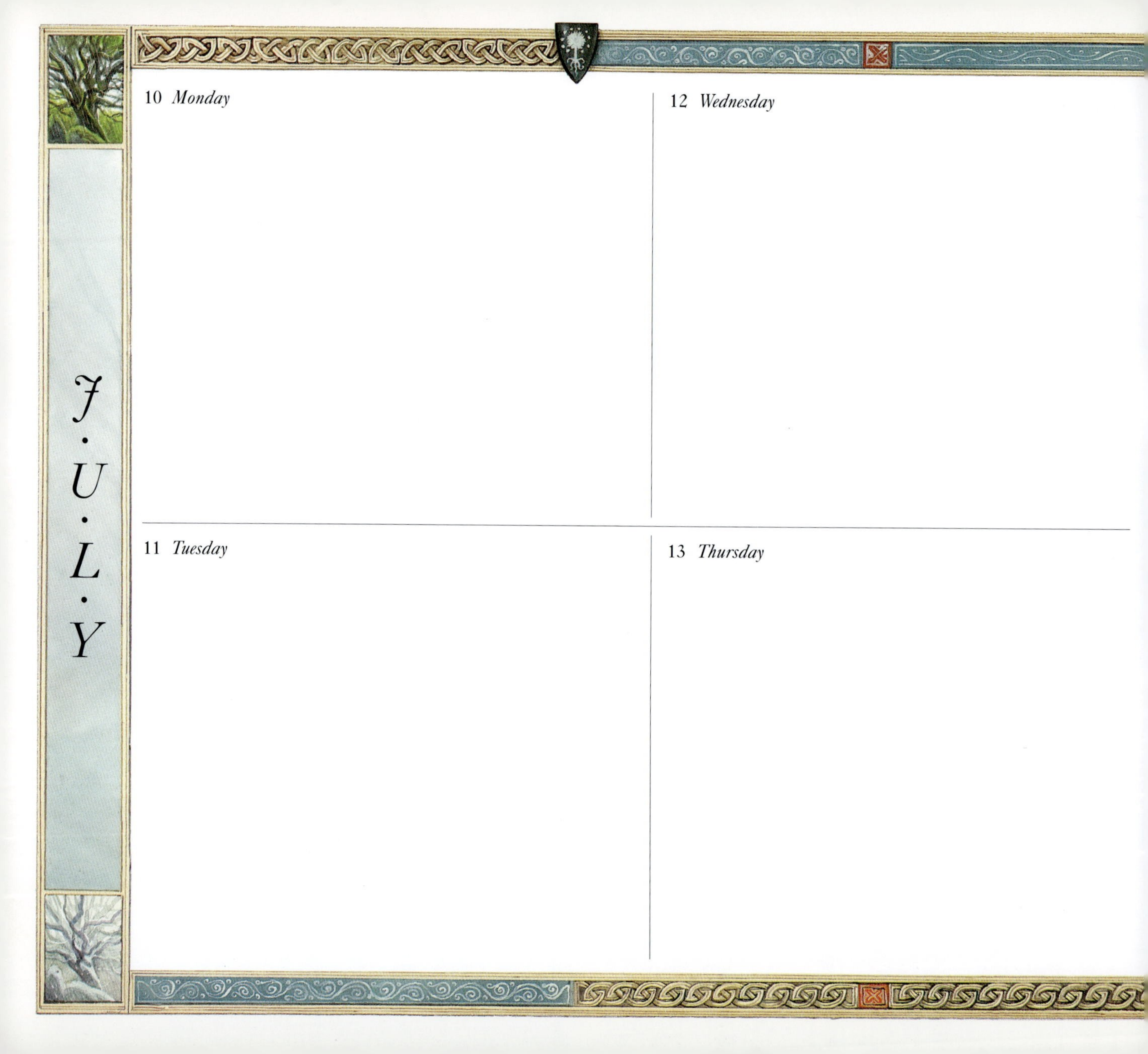

J · U · L · Y

10 *Monday*

12 *Wednesday*

11 *Tuesday*

13 *Thursday*

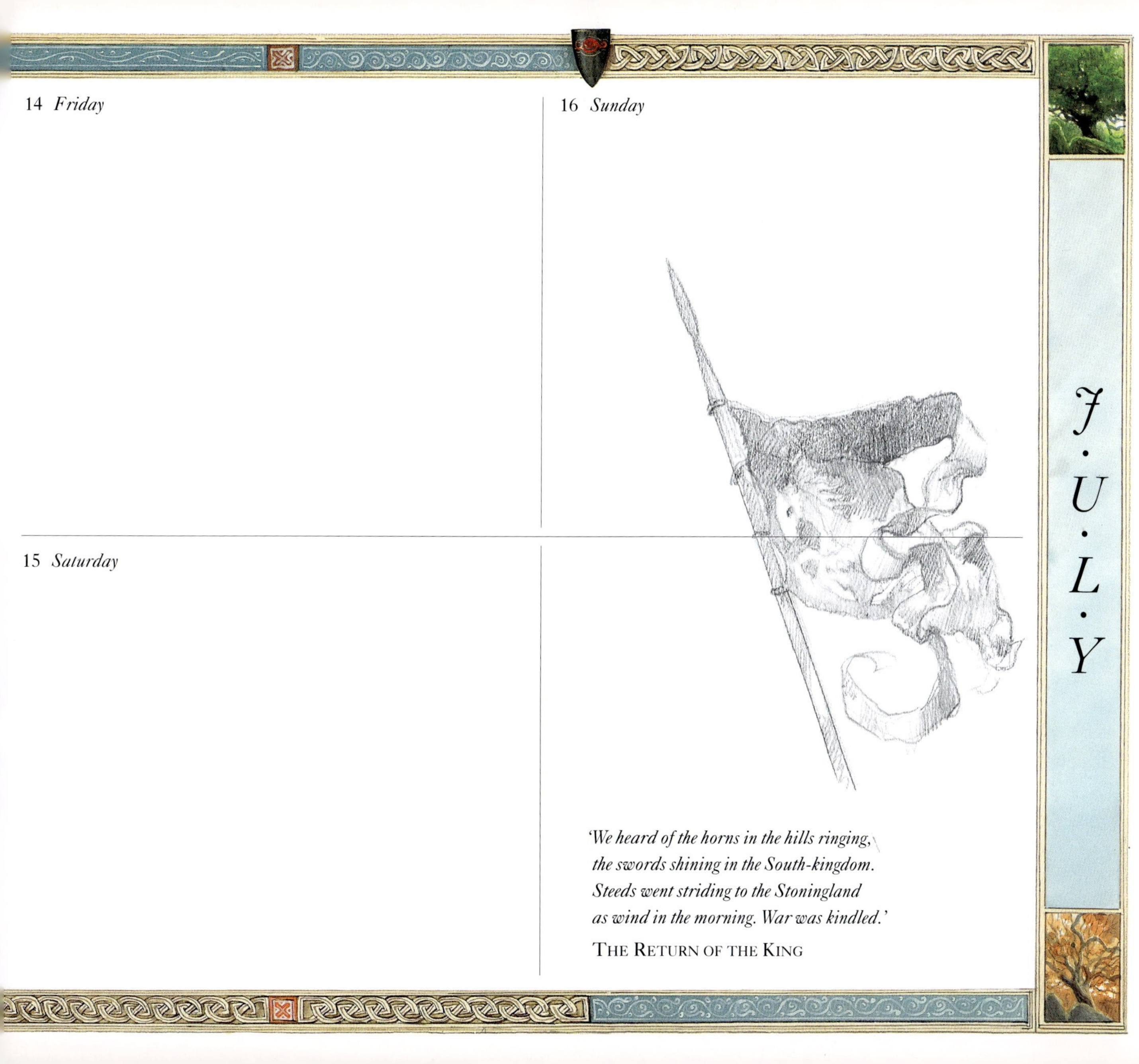

14 *Friday*

15 *Saturday*

16 *Sunday*

'We heard of the horns in the hills ringing,
the swords shining in the South-kingdom.
Steeds went striding to the Stoningland
as wind in the morning. War was kindled.'

THE RETURN OF THE KING

17 *Monday*

19 *Wednesday*

18 *Tuesday*

20 *Thursday*

On July 18th S.R. 1419 Éomer returned to Minas Tirith

21 Friday
23 Sunday
22 Saturday
J·U·L·Y

24 *Monday*

25 *Tuesday*

26 *Wednesday*

27 *Thursday*

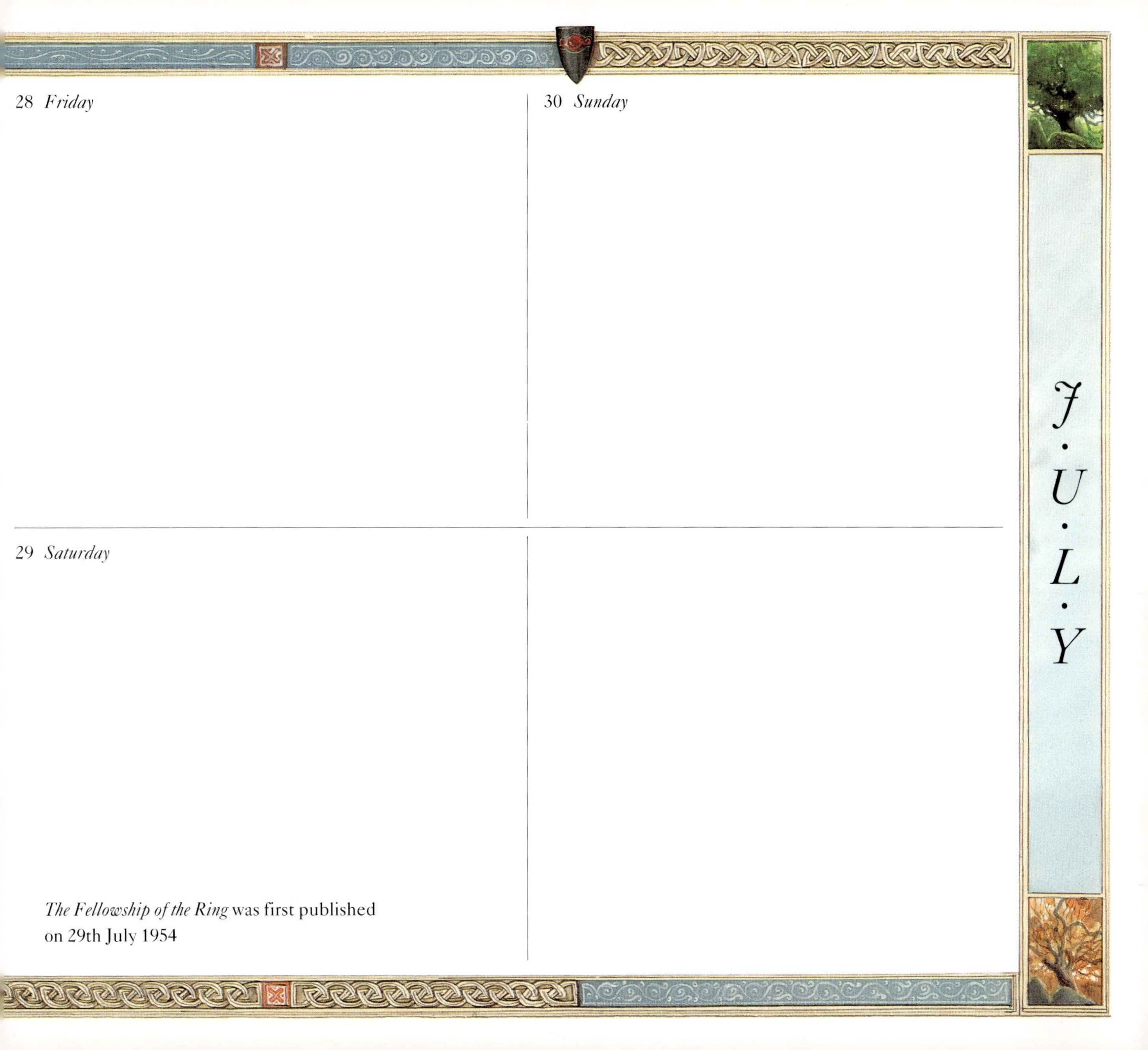

28 *Friday*

30 *Sunday*

29 *Saturday*

The Fellowship of the Ring was first published on 29th July 1954

J · U · L · Y

A·U·G·U·S·T

31 *Monday*

1 *Tuesday*

2 *Wednesday*

3 *Thursday*

OLD MAN WILLOW

A·U·G·U·S·T

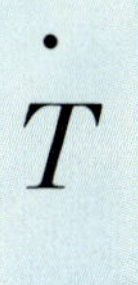

4 *Friday*

5 *Saturday*

6 *Sunday*

During August S.R. 1419 all trace of Gollum was lost.
It was thought that he had taken refuge in Moria;
but when he at last discovered the way to the West-gate
he could not get out.

AUGUST

7 *Monday*

8 *Tuesday*

9 *Wednesday*

10 *Thursday*

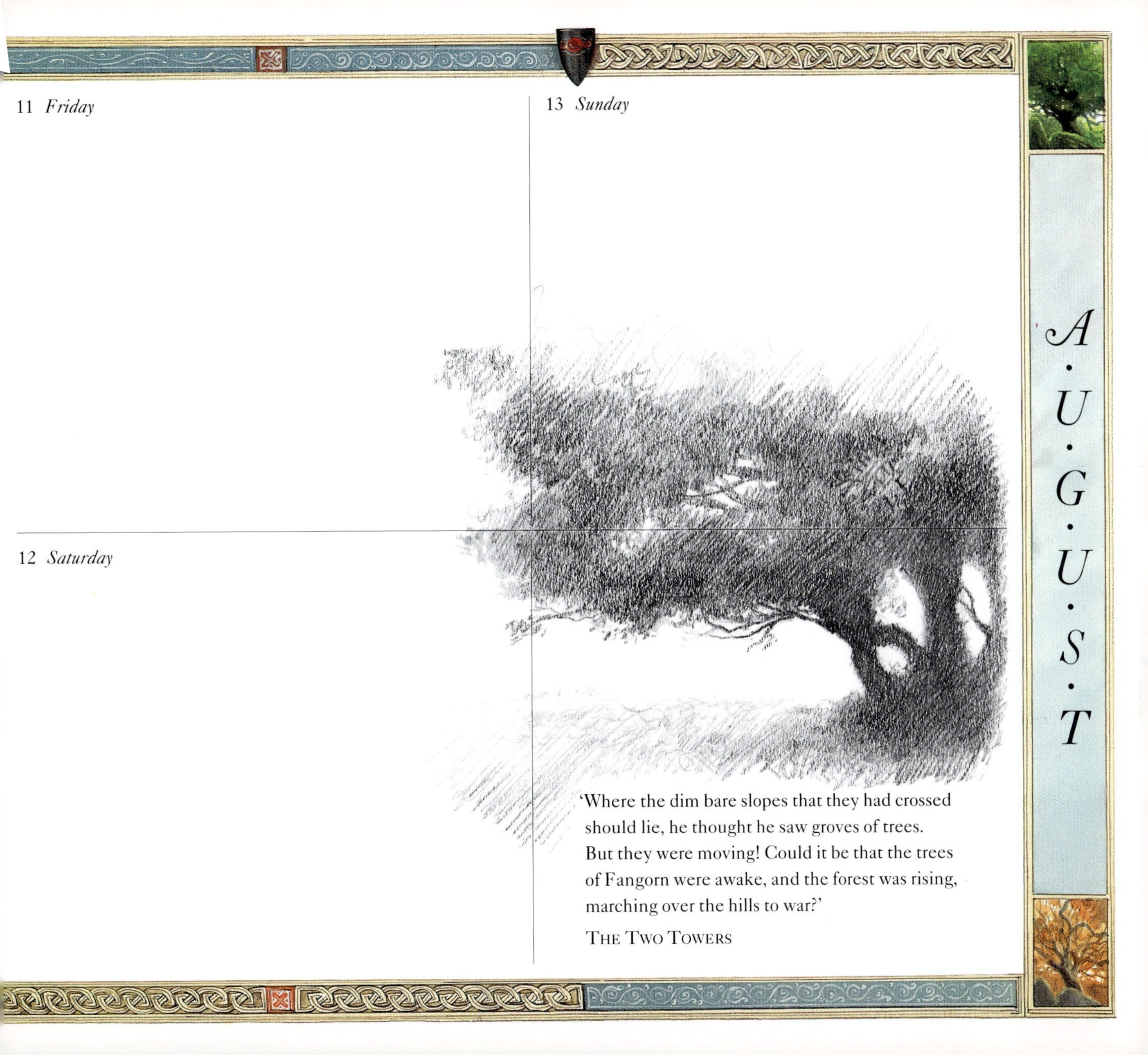

11 *Friday*

12 *Saturday*

13 *Sunday*

'Where the dim bare slopes that they had crossed should lie, he thought he saw groves of trees. But they were moving! Could it be that the trees of Fangorn were awake, and the forest was rising, marching over the hills to war?'

THE TWO TOWERS

A·U·G·U·S·T

14 *Monday*

15 *Tuesday*

16 *Wednesday*

17 *Thursday*

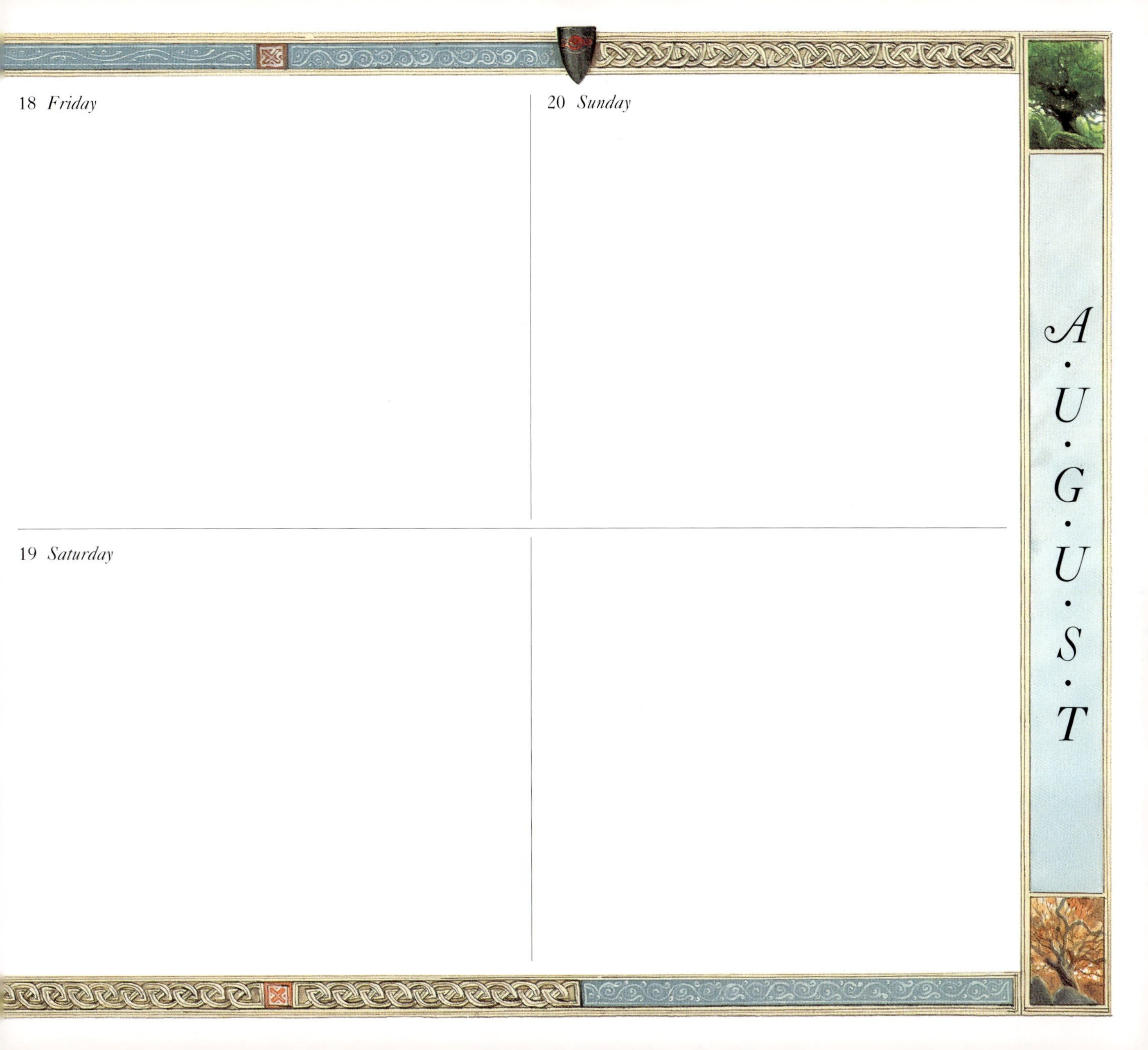

18 *Friday*

20 *Sunday*

19 *Saturday*

A·U·G·U·S·T

AUGUST

21 *Monday*

23 *Wednesday*

22 *Tuesday*

24 *Thursday*

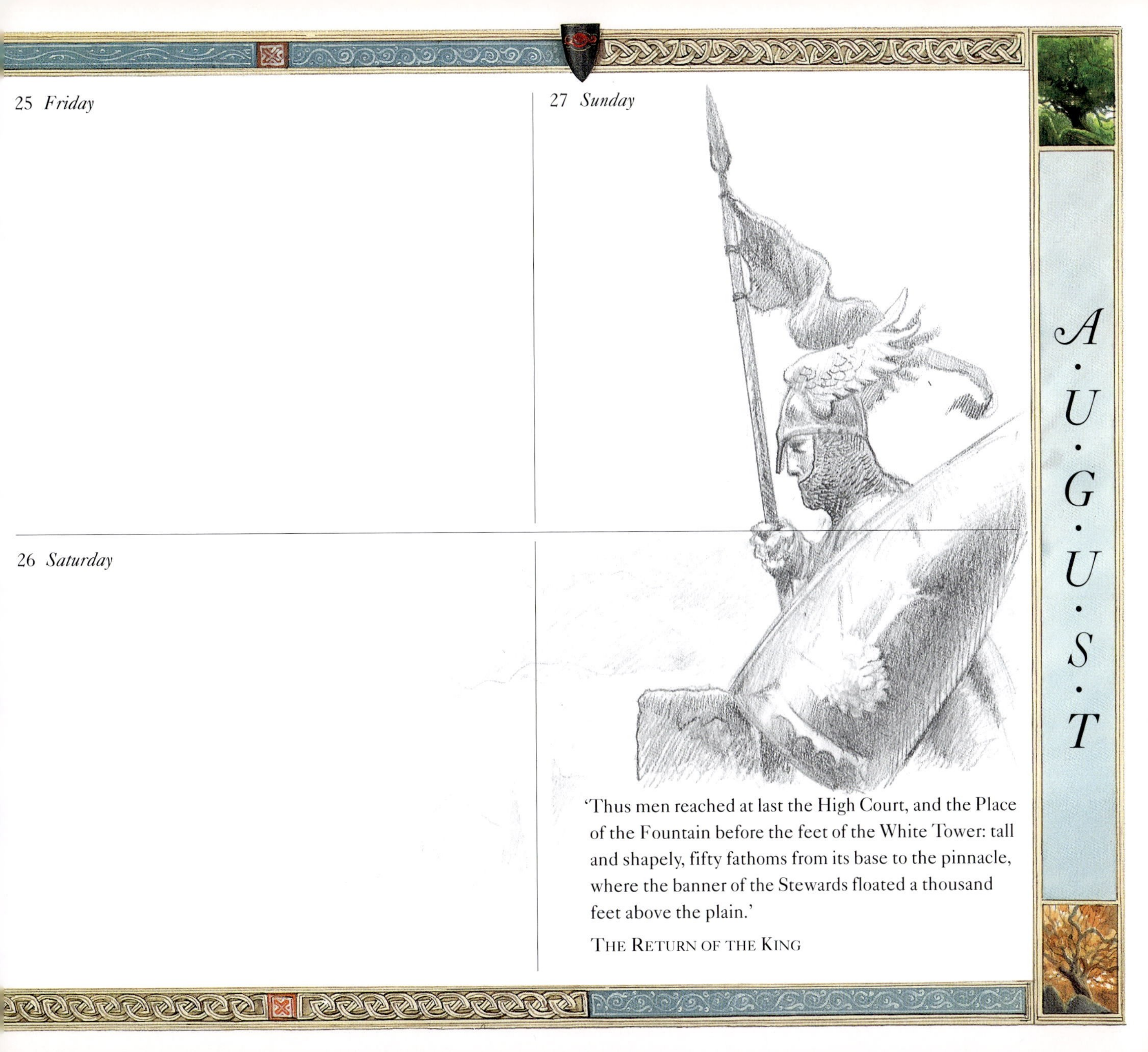

25 *Friday*

26 *Saturday*

27 *Sunday*

'Thus men reached at last the High Court, and the Place of the Fountain before the feet of the White Tower: tall and shapely, fifty fathoms from its base to the pinnacle, where the banner of the Stewards floated a thousand feet above the plain.'

THE RETURN OF THE KING

A · U · G · U · S · T

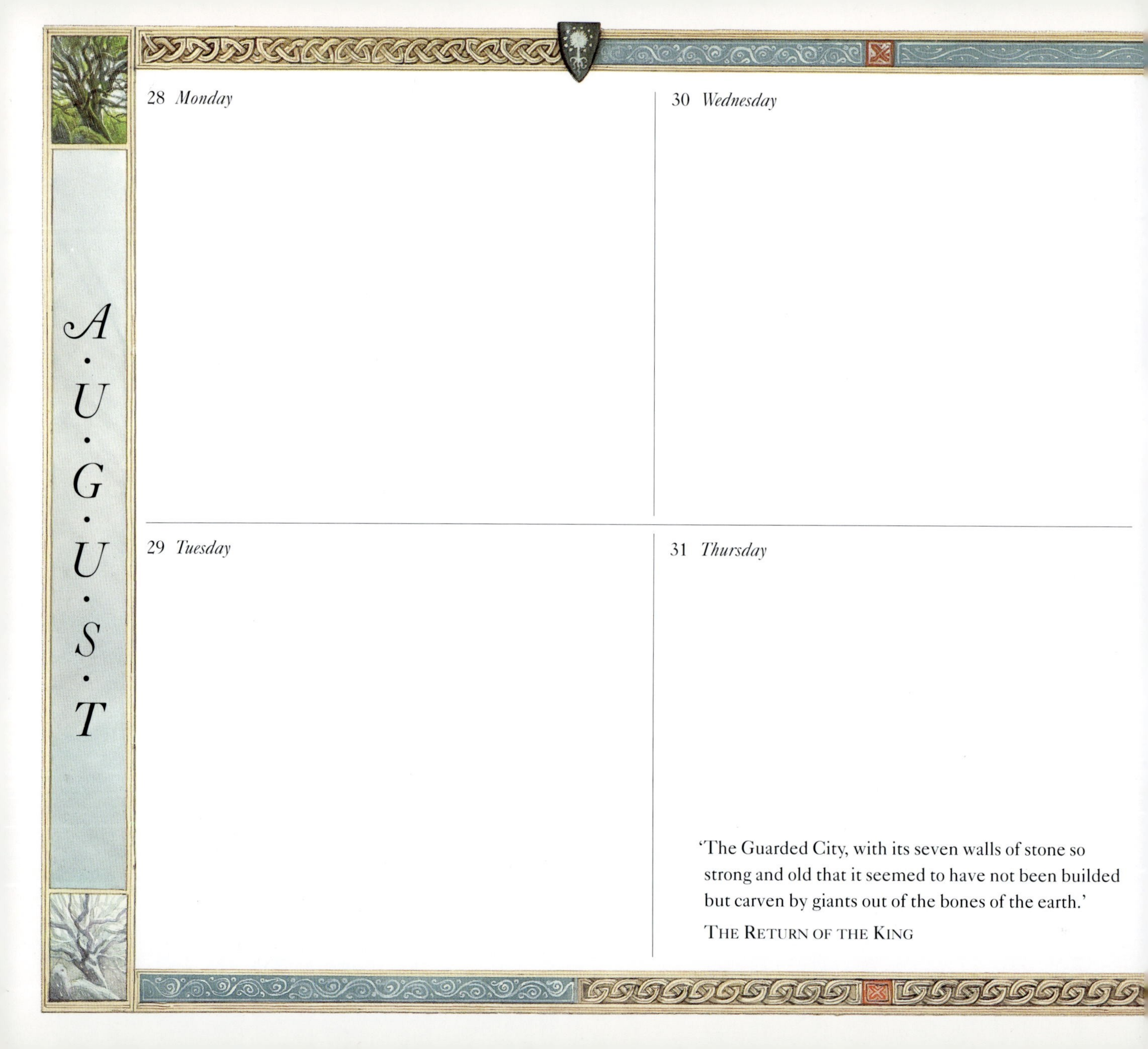

A·U·G·U·S·T

28 *Monday*

29 *Tuesday*

30 *Wednesday*

31 *Thursday*

‘The Guarded City, with its seven walls of stone so strong and old that it seemed to have not been builded but carven by giants out of the bones of the earth.’

THE RETURN OF THE KING

S·E·P·T·E·M·B·E·R

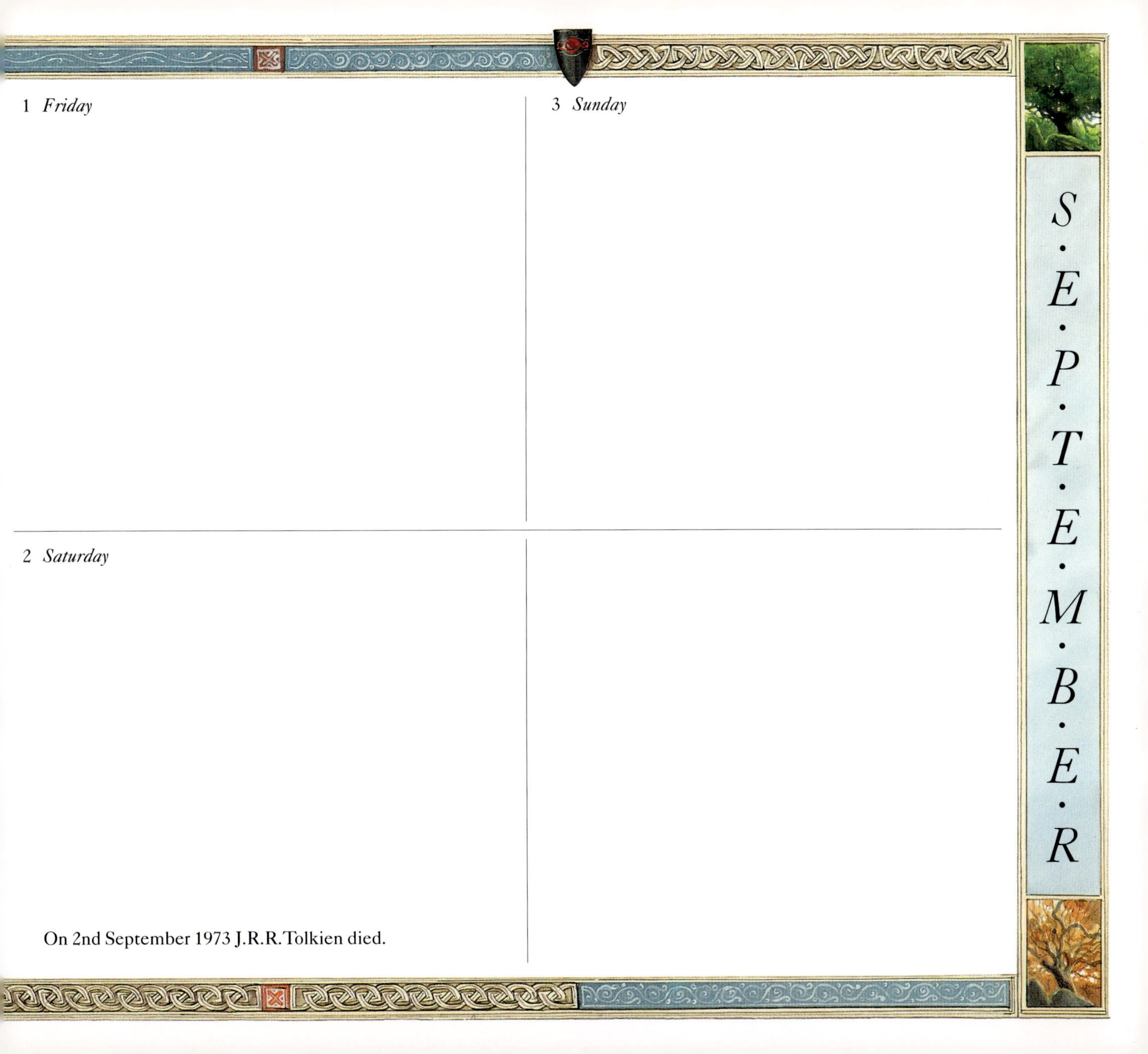

1 *Friday*

2 *Saturday*

On 2nd September 1973 J.R.R.Tolkien died.

3 *Sunday*

S·E·P·T·E·M·B·E·R

S·E·P·T·E·M·B·E·R

4 *Monday*

6 *Wednesday*

5 *Tuesday*

7 *Thursday*

8 *Friday*

9 *Saturday*

10 *Sunday*

On 10th September S.R. 1418 Gandalf escaped from Orthanc.

S·E·P·T·E·M·B·E·R

S·E·P·T·E·M·B·E·R

11 *Monday*

12 *Tuesday*

13 *Wednesday*

14 *Thursday*

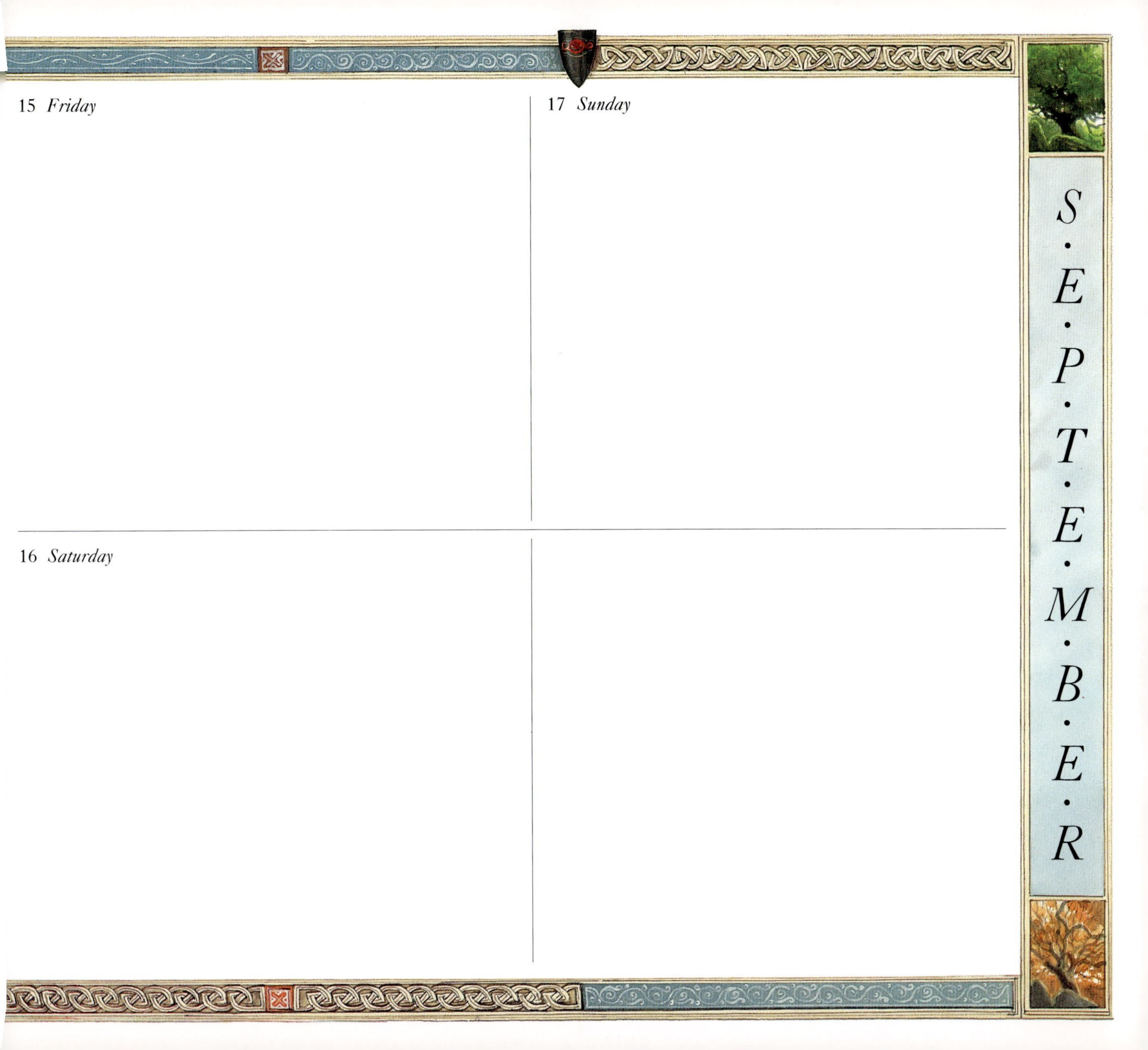

15 *Friday*

16 *Saturday*

17 *Sunday*

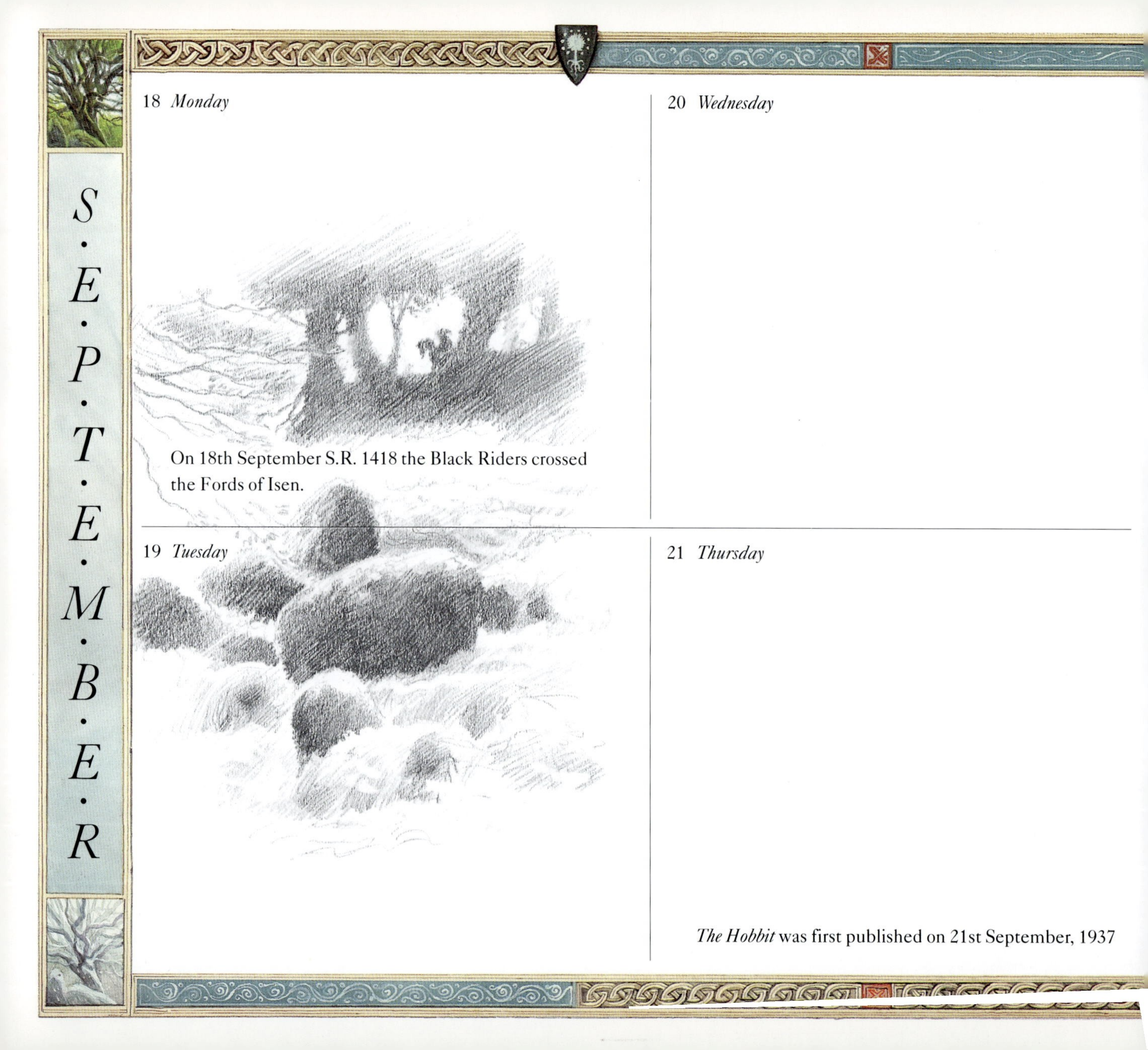

18 *Monday*

On 18th September S.R. 1418 the Black Riders crossed the Fords of Isen.

19 *Tuesday*

20 *Wednesday*

21 *Thursday*

The Hobbit was first published on 21st September, 1937

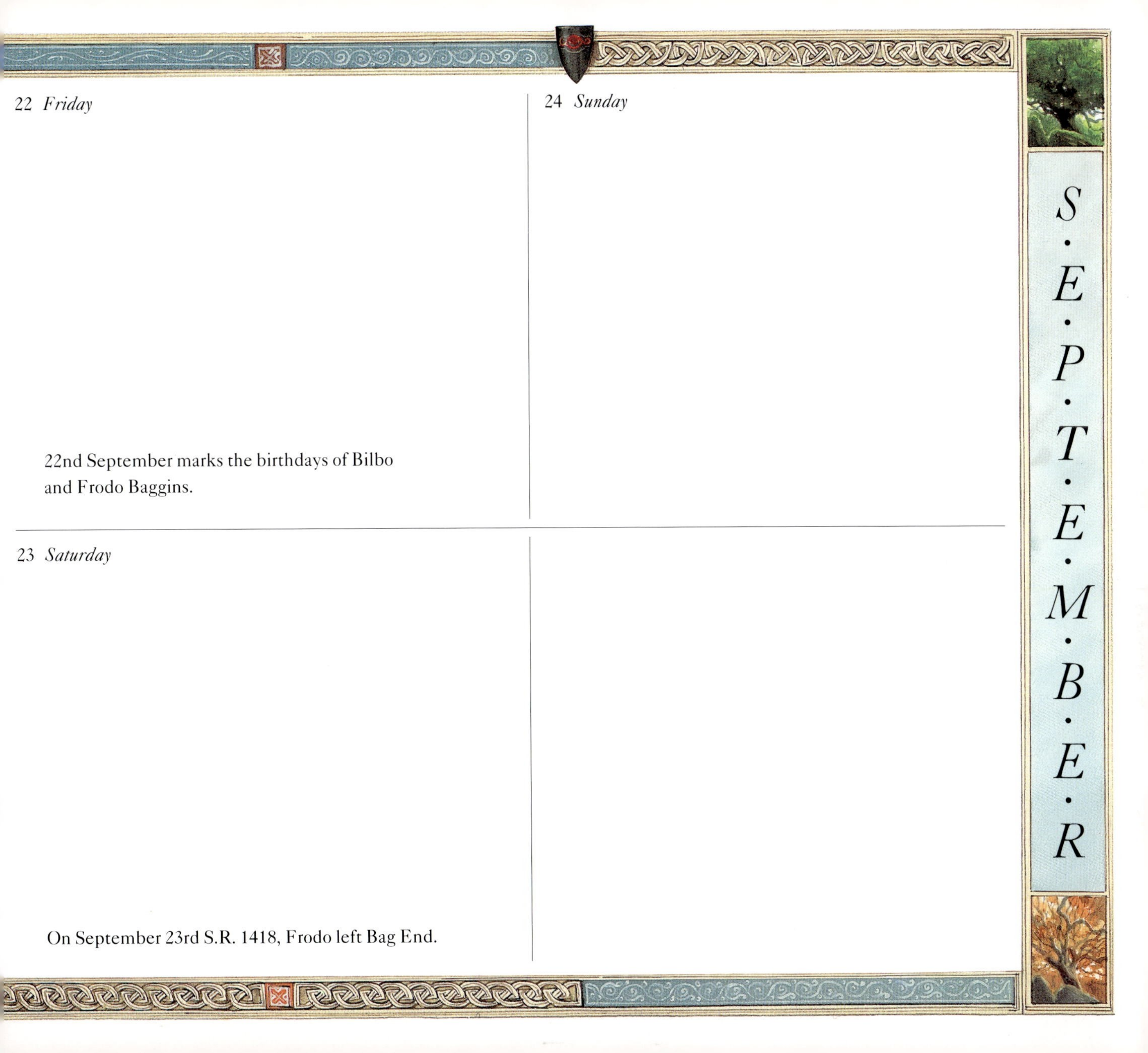

22 *Friday*

22nd September marks the birthdays of Bilbo and Frodo Baggins.

23 *Saturday*

On September 23rd S.R. 1418, Frodo left Bag End.

24 *Sunday*

S·E·P·T·E·M·B·E·R

25 *Monday*

26 *Tuesday*

27 *Wednesday*

28 *Thursday*

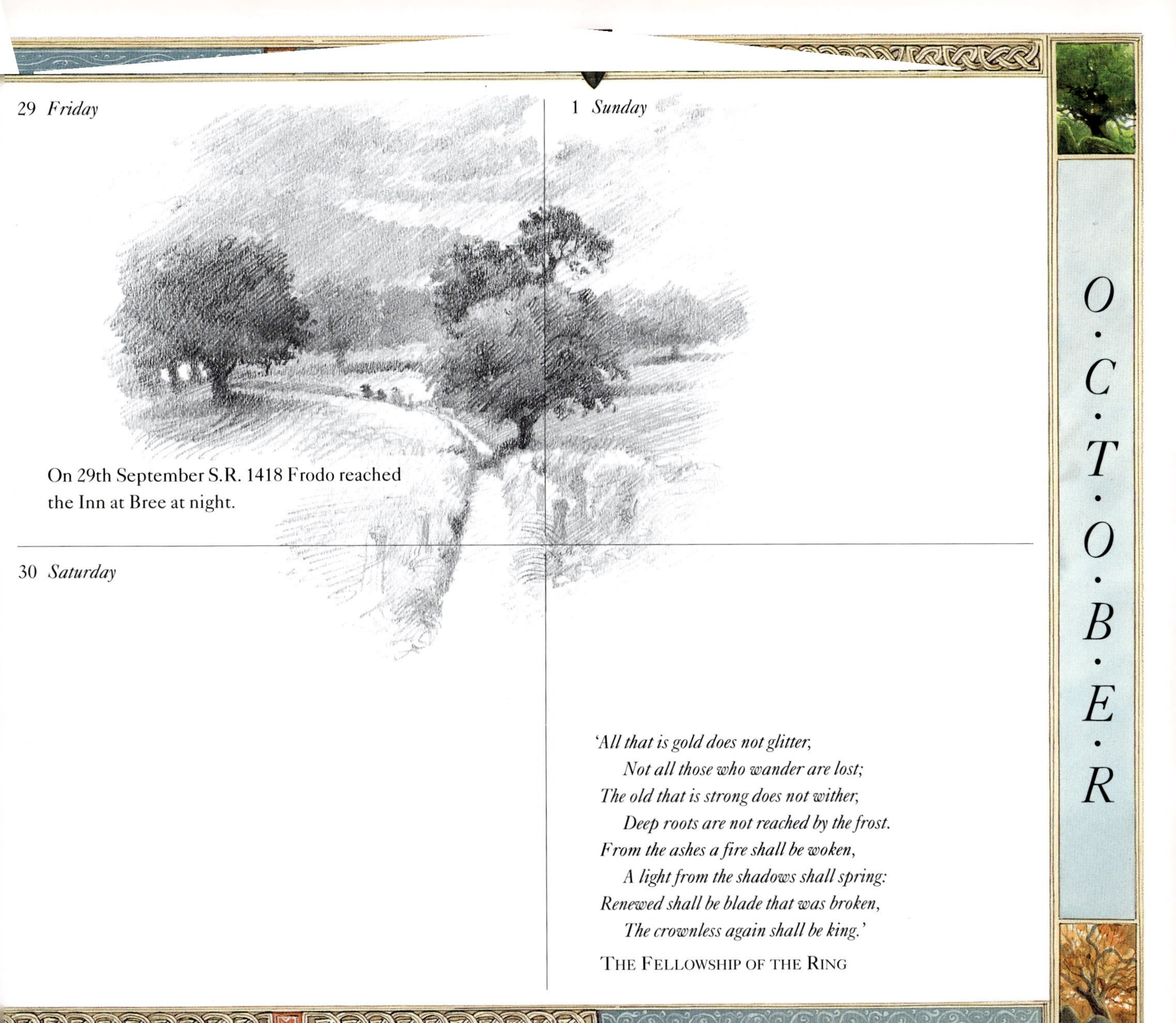

29 *Friday*

On 29th September S.R. 1418 Frodo reached the Inn at Bree at night.

30 *Saturday*

1 *Sunday*

'All that is gold does not glitter,
Not all those who wander are lost;
The old that is strong does not wither,
Deep roots are not reached by the frost.
From the ashes a fire shall be woken,
A light from the shadows shall spring:
Renewed shall be blade that was broken,
The crownless again shall be king.'

THE FELLOWSHIP OF THE RING

O·C·T·O·B·E·R

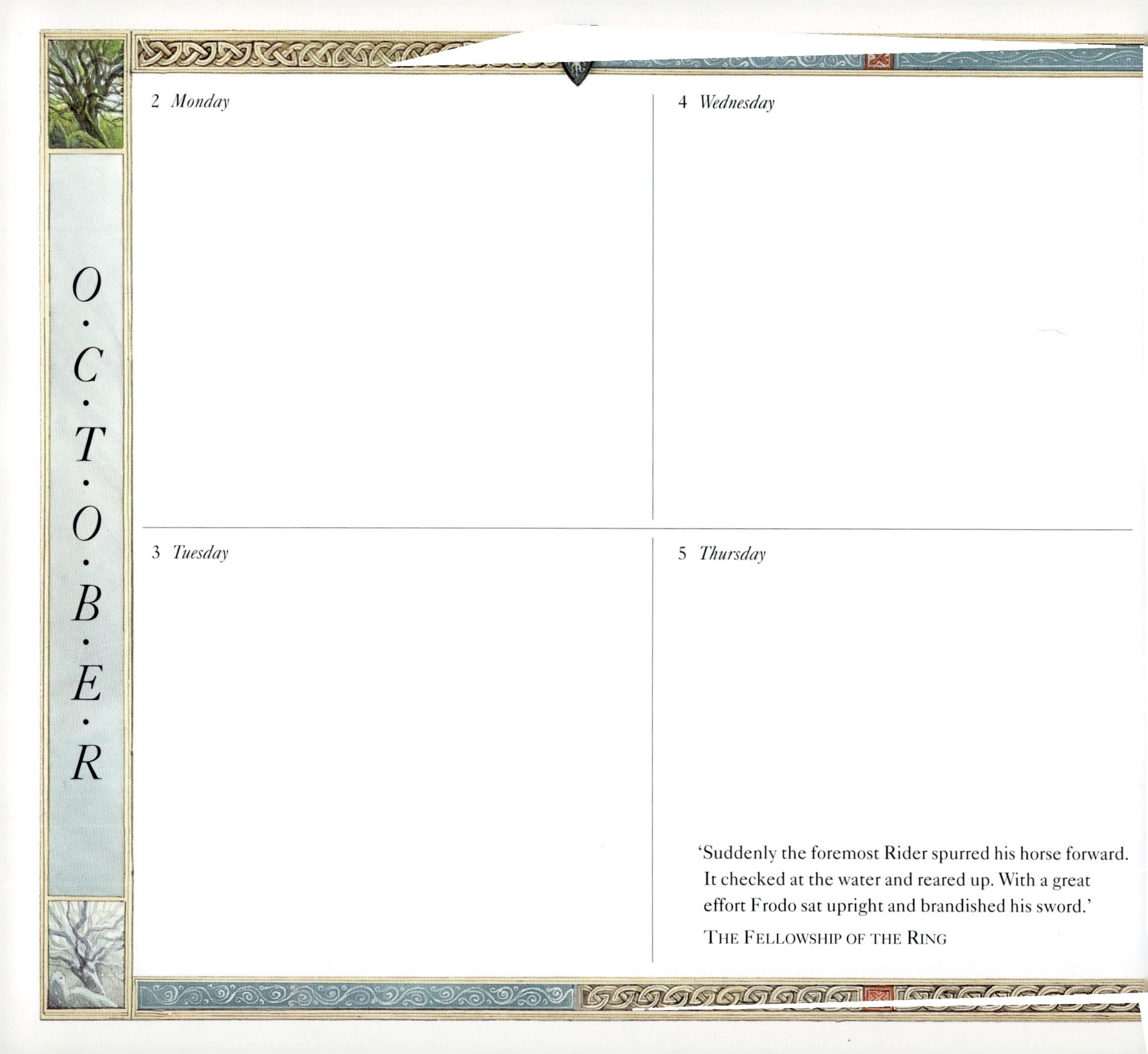

2 *Monday*

3 *Tuesday*

4 *Wednesday*

5 *Thursday*

'Suddenly the foremost Rider spurred his horse forward. It checked at the water and reared up. With a great effort Frodo sat upright and brandished his sword.'

THE FELLOWSHIP OF THE RING

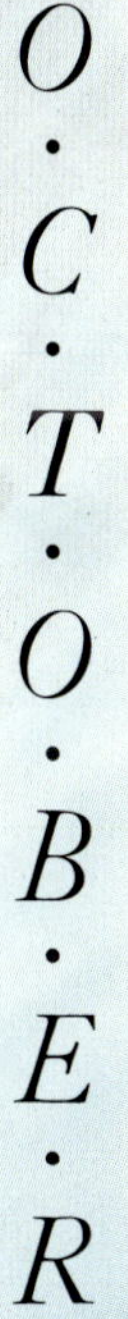
O·C·T·O·B·E·R

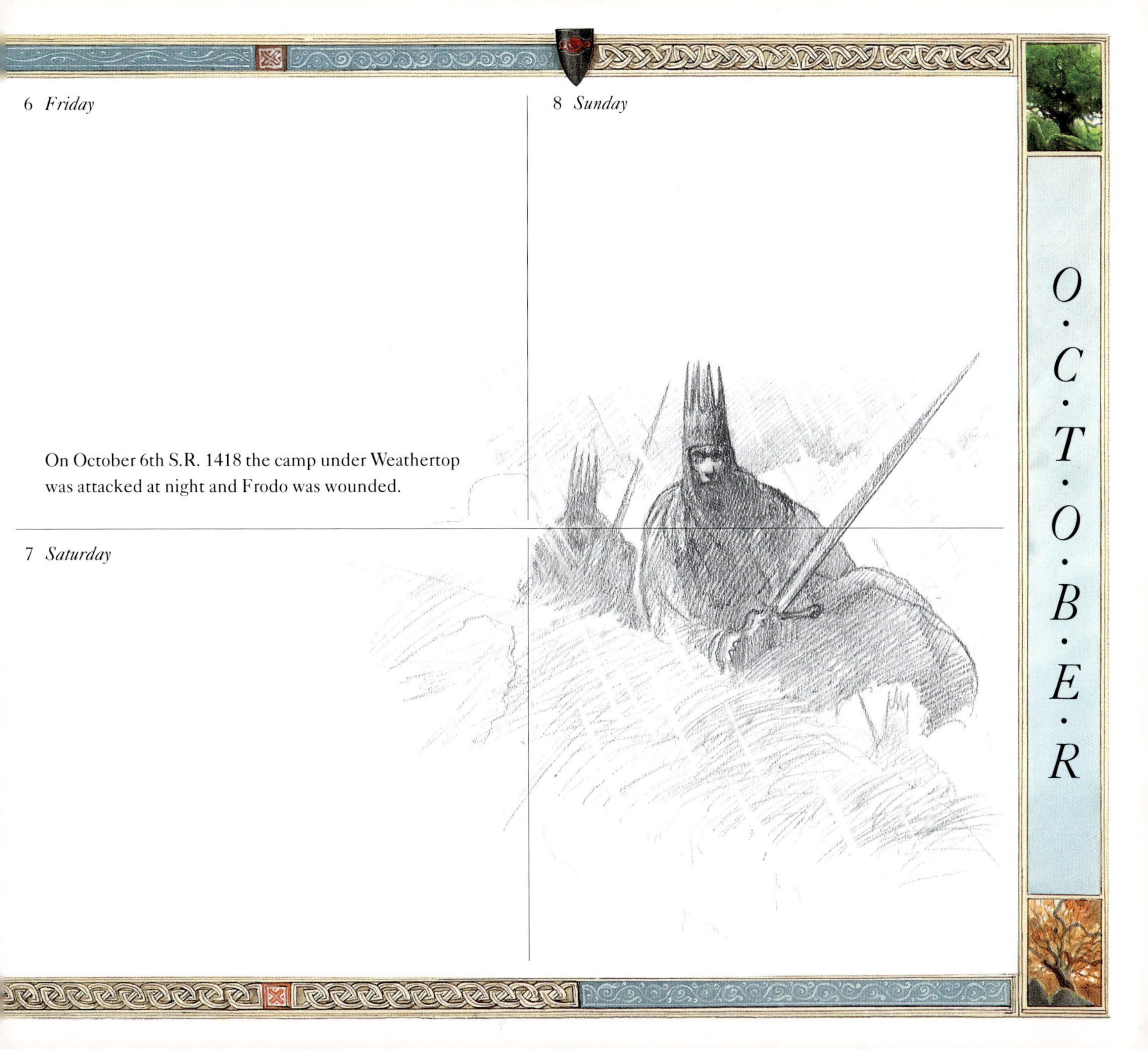

6 *Friday*

On October 6th S.R. 1418 the camp under Weathertop was attacked at night and Frodo was wounded.

7 *Saturday*

8 *Sunday*

O·C·T·O·B·E·R

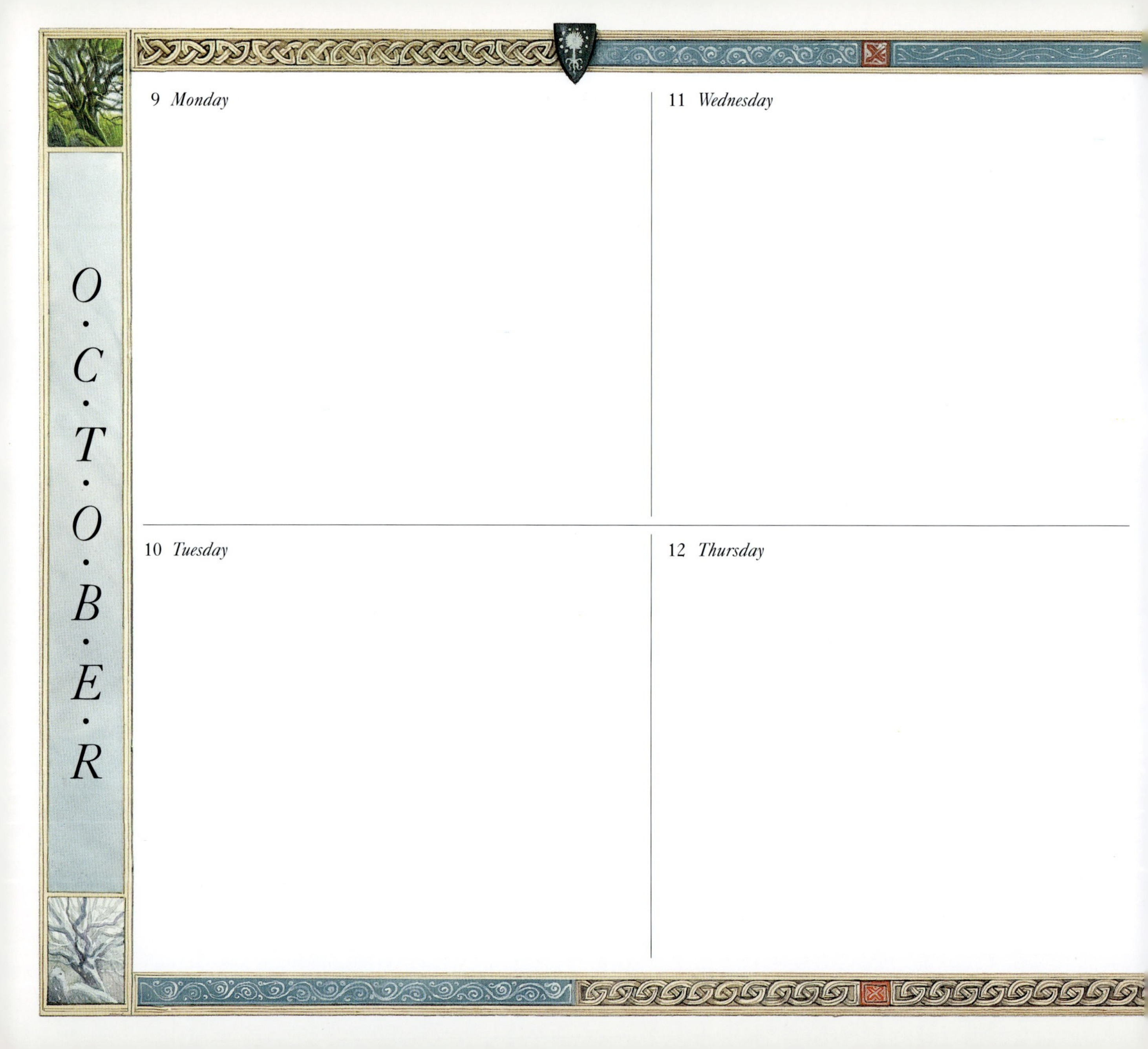

O·C·T·O·B·E·R

9 *Monday*

10 *Tuesday*

11 *Wednesday*

12 *Thursday*

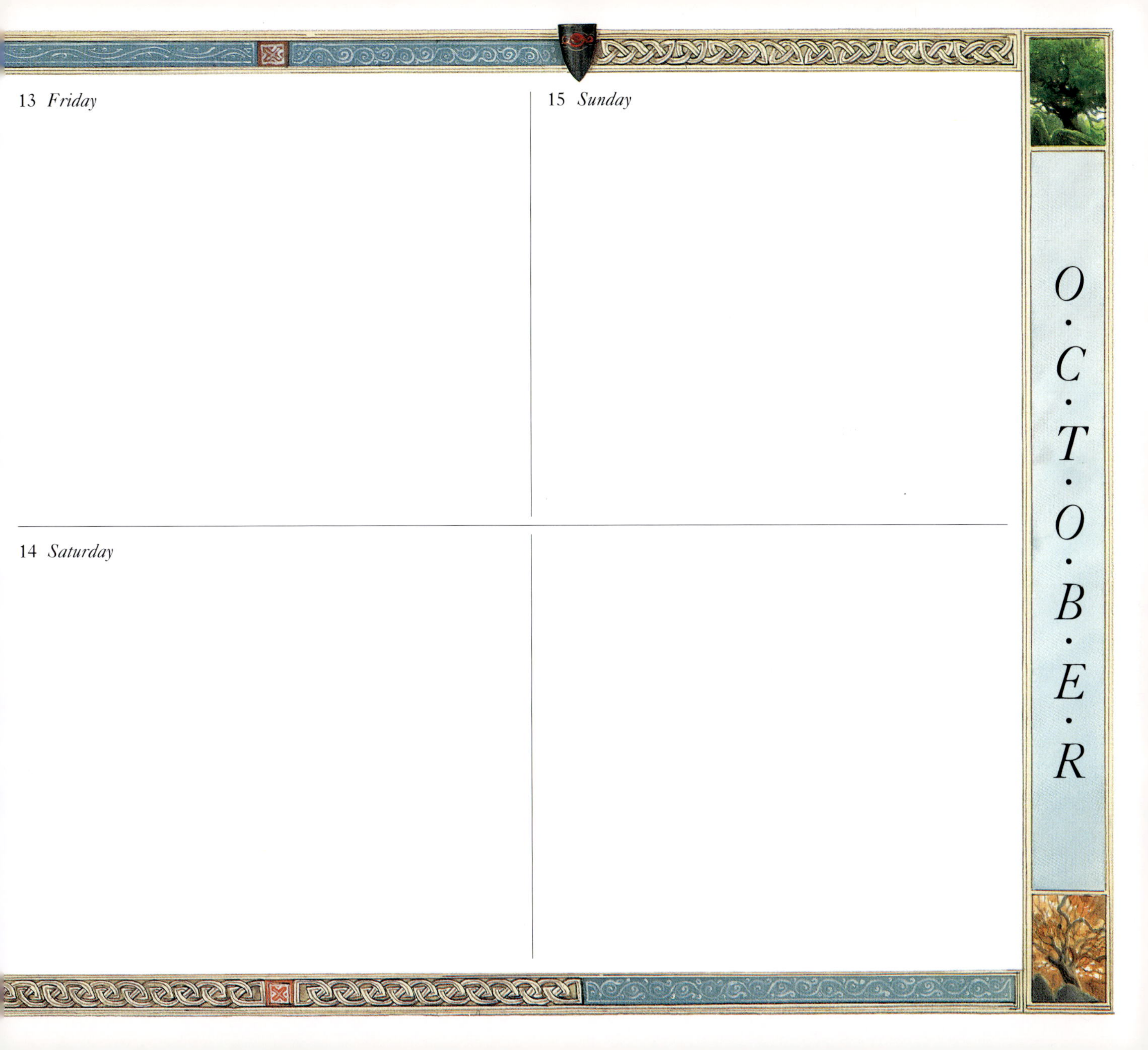

13 *Friday*

15 *Sunday*

14 *Saturday*

O·C·T·O·B·E·R

O·C·T·O·B·E·R

16 *Monday*

17 *Tuesday*

18 *Wednesday*

On 18th October S.R. 1418 Glorfindel found Frodo, cold and wounded, at dusk after the attack at Weathertop

19 *Thursday*

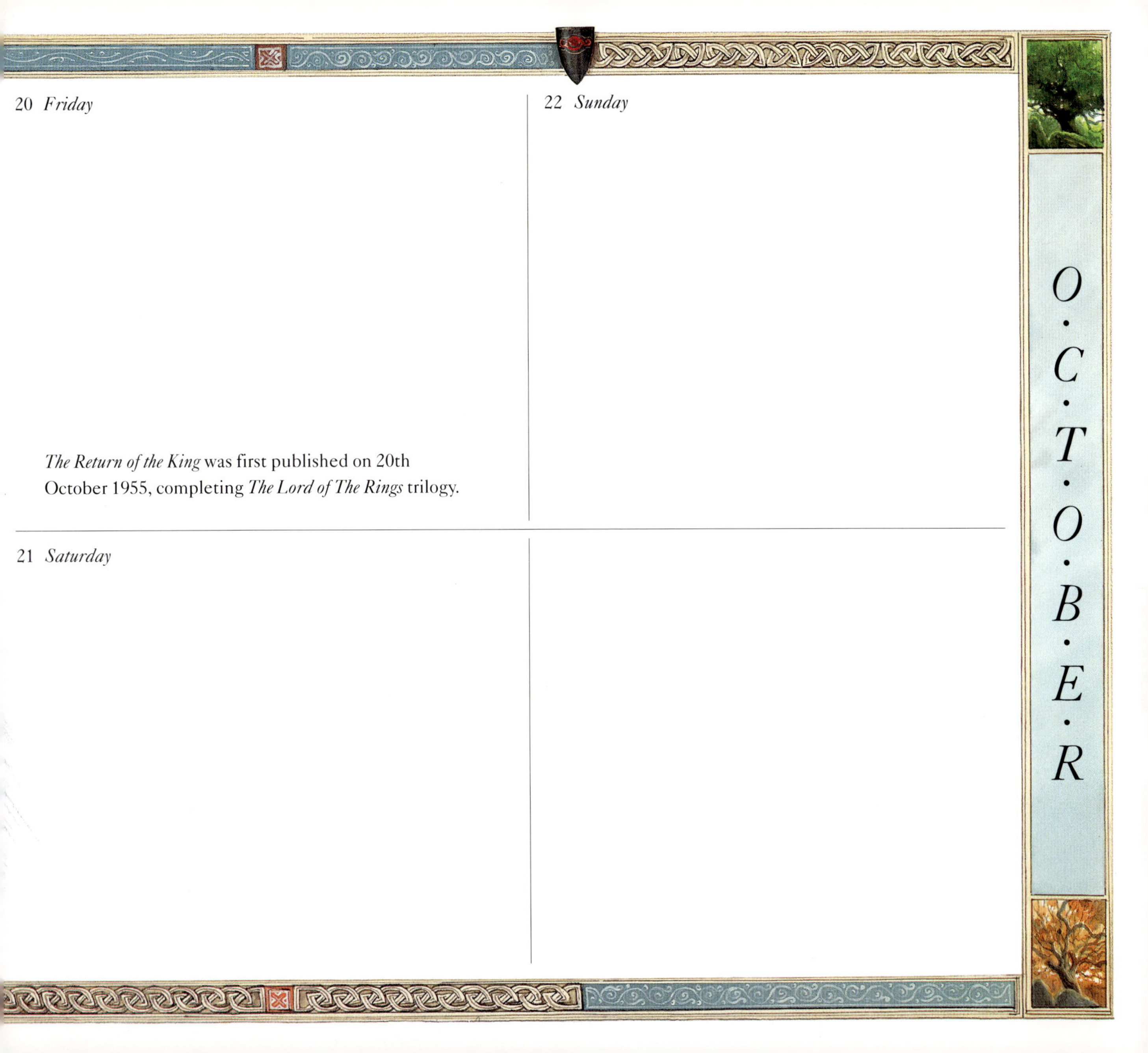

20 *Friday*

The Return of the King was first published on 20th October 1955, completing *The Lord of The Rings* trilogy.

21 *Saturday*

22 *Sunday*

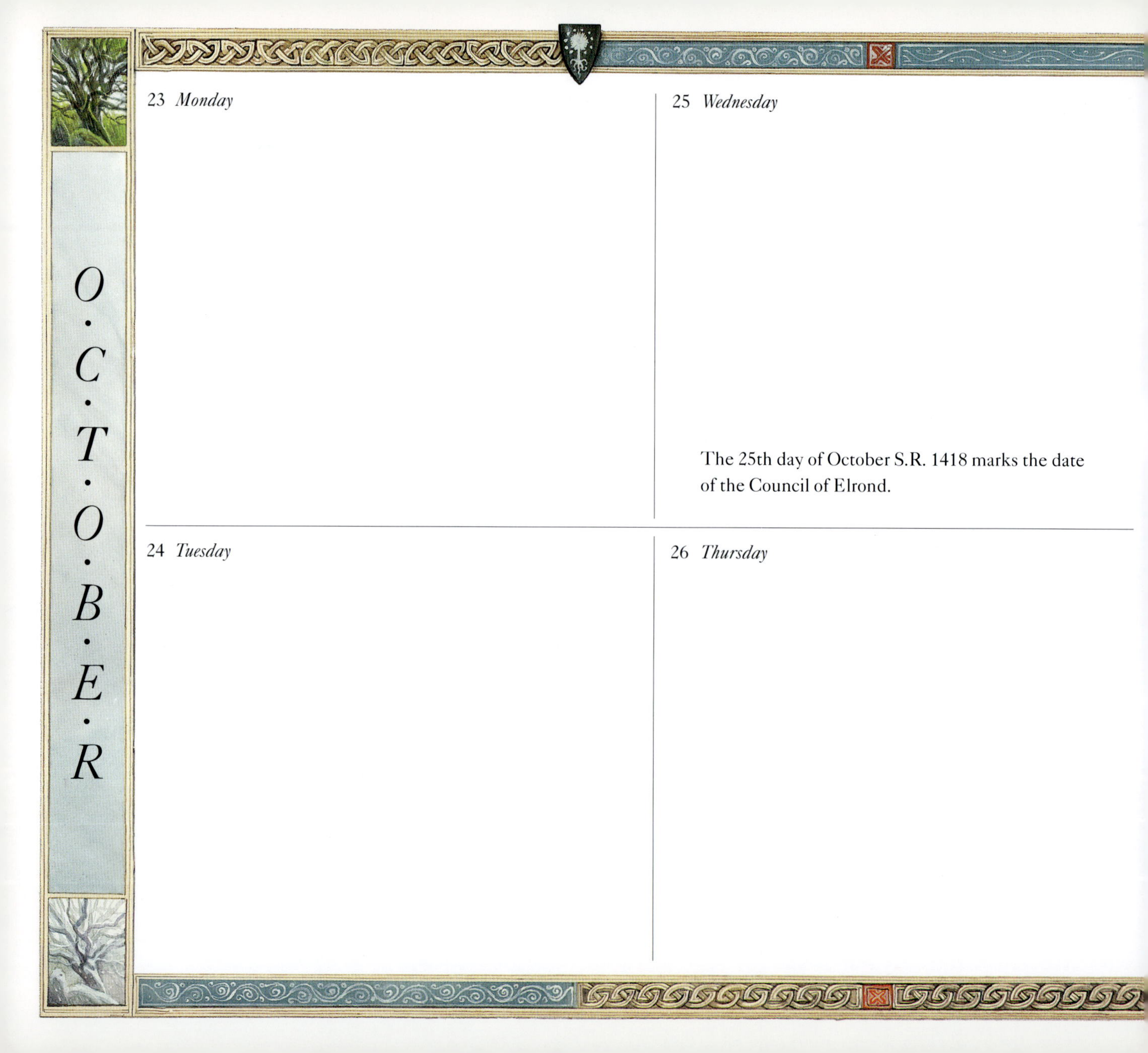

23 *Monday*

24 *Tuesday*

25 *Wednesday*

The 25th day of October S.R. 1418 marks the date of the Council of Elrond.

26 *Thursday*

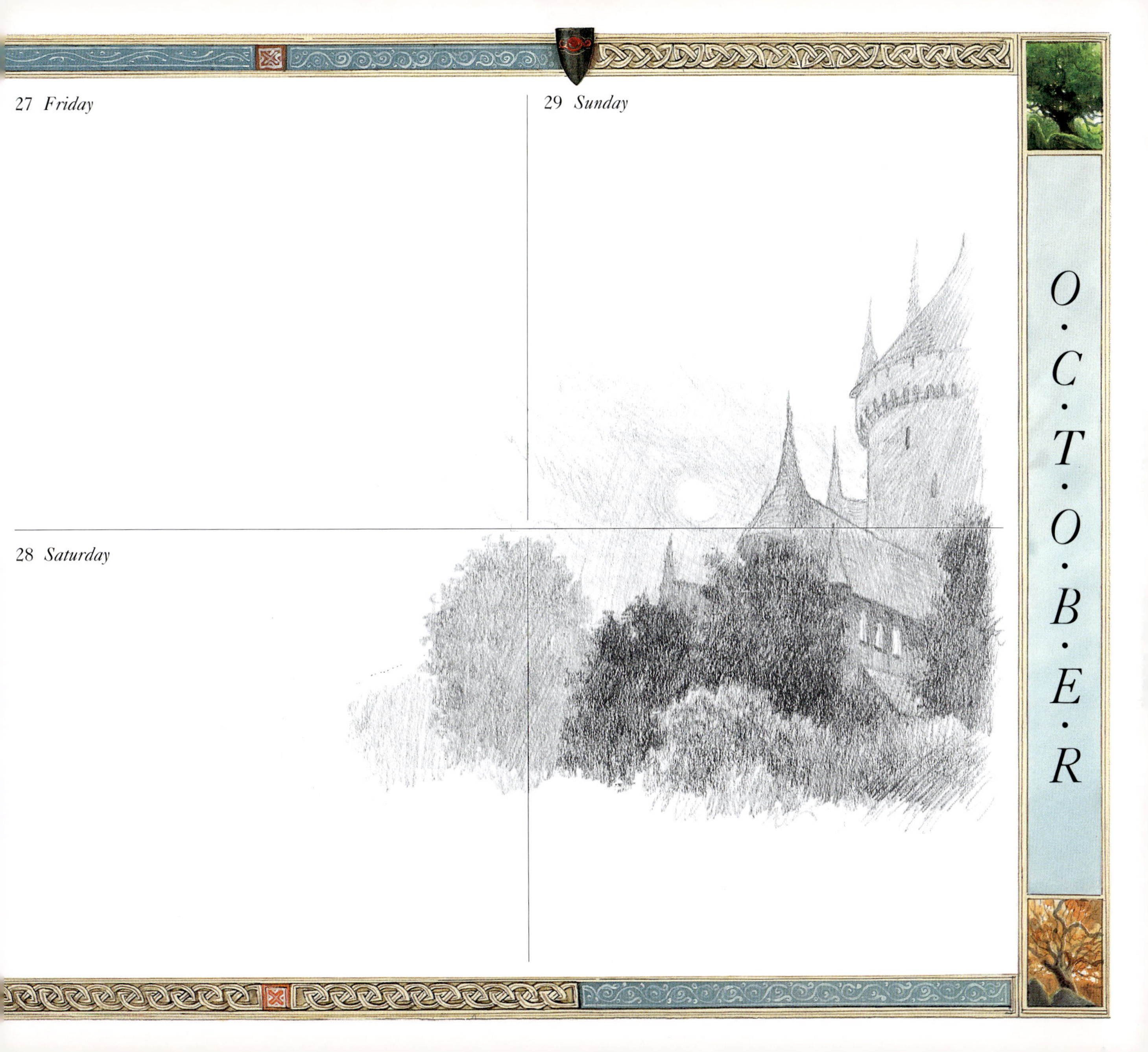

27 *Friday*

28 *Saturday*

29 *Sunday*

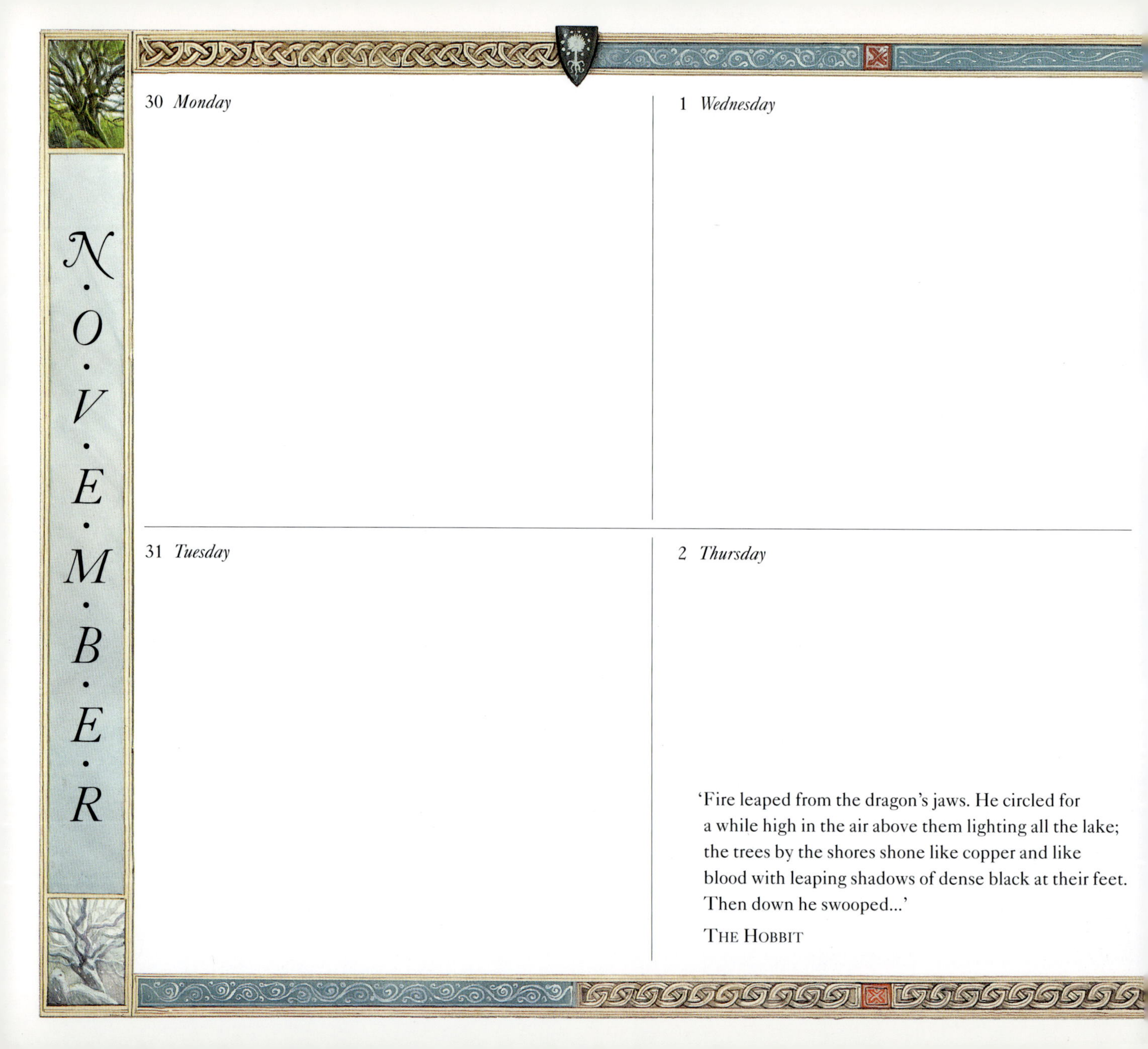

30 *Monday*

31 *Tuesday*

1 *Wednesday*

2 *Thursday*

'Fire leaped from the dragon's jaws. He circled for a while high in the air above them lighting all the lake; the trees by the shores shone like copper and like blood with leaping shadows of dense black at their feet. Then down he swooped...'

THE HOBBIT

N·O·V·E·M·B·E·R

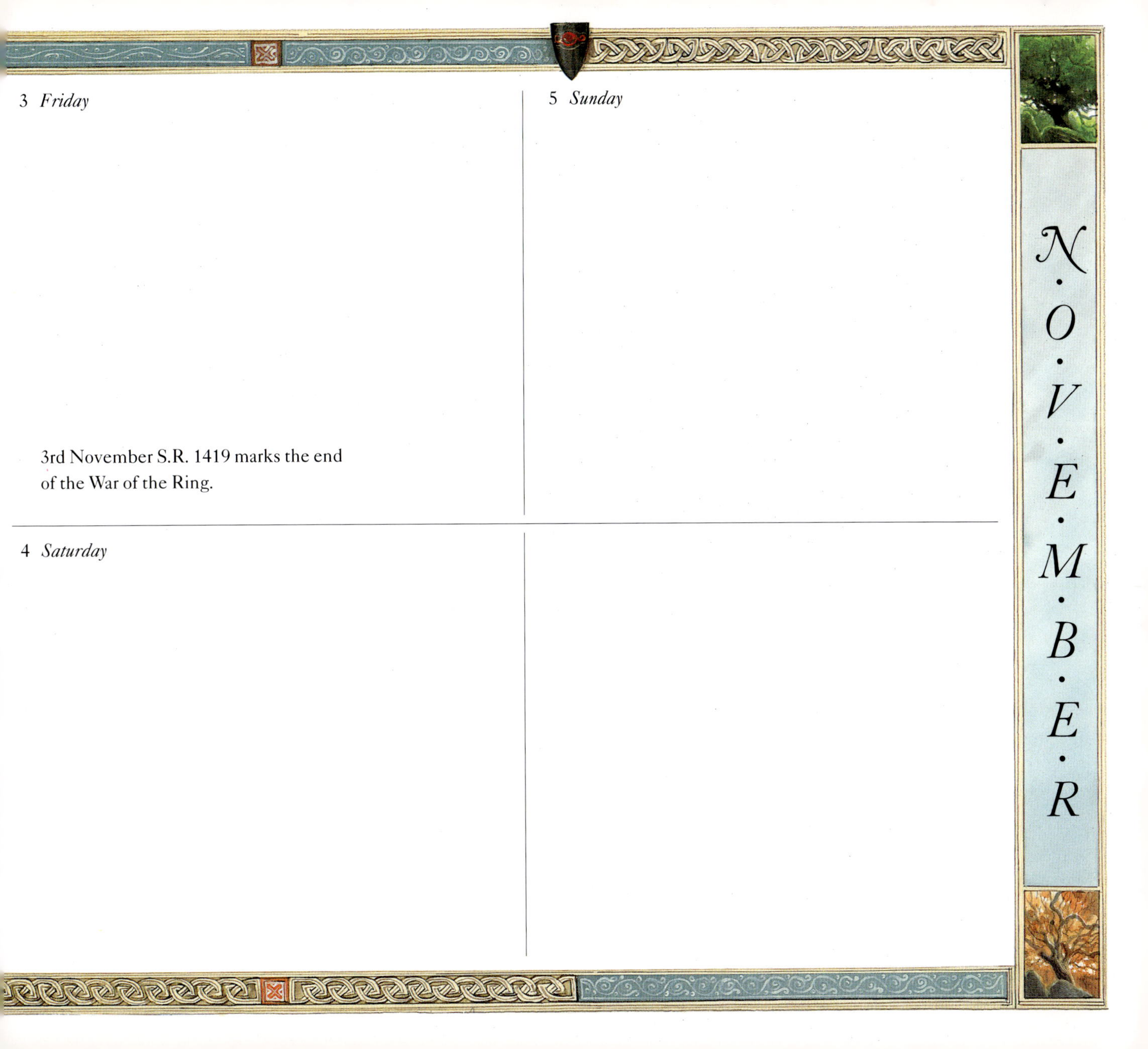

3 *Friday*

3rd November S.R. 1419 marks the end of the War of the Ring.

4 *Saturday*

5 *Sunday*

6 *Monday*

7 *Tuesday*

8 *Wednesday*

9 *Thursday*

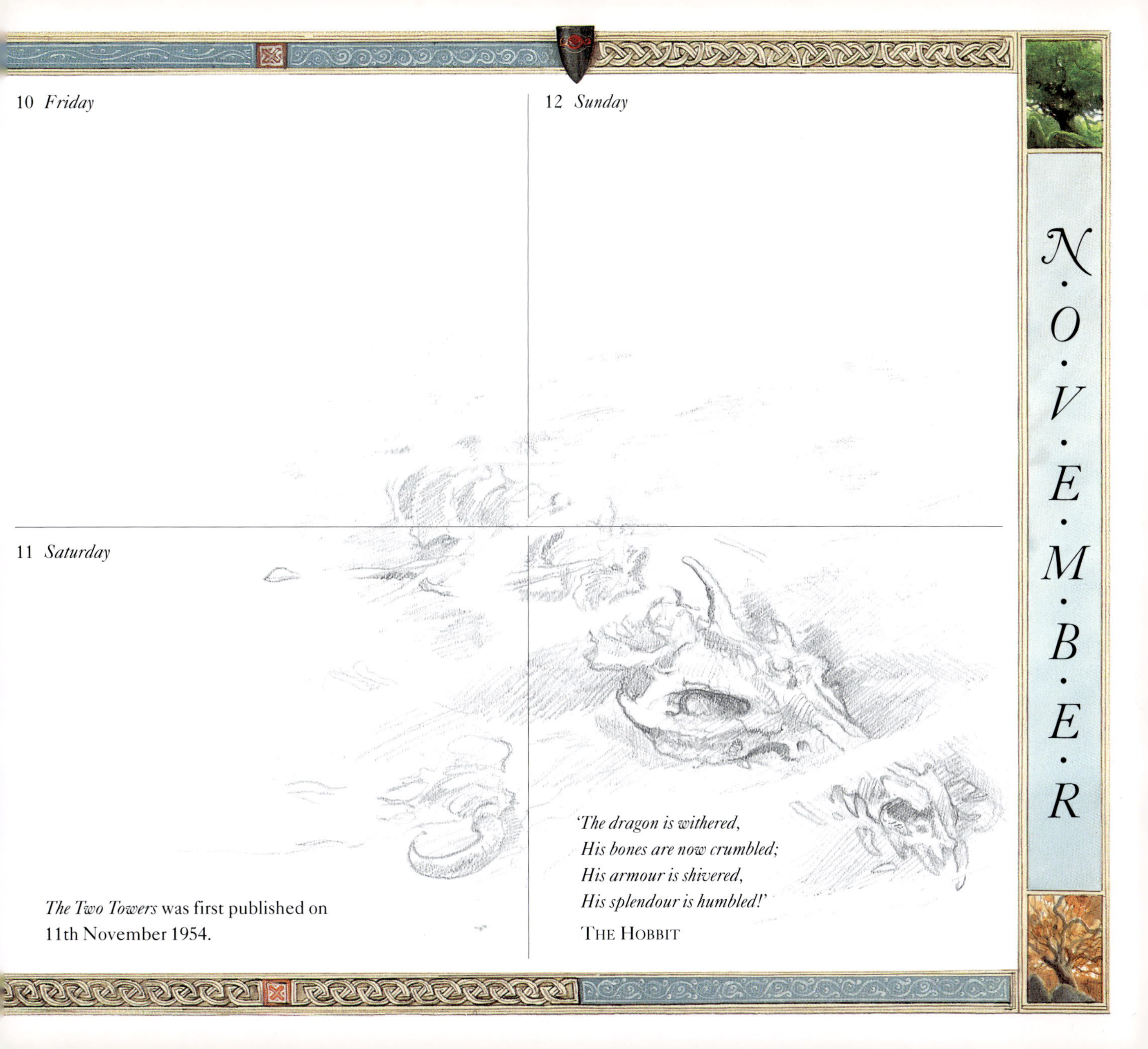

10 *Friday*

11 *Saturday*

The Two Towers was first published on 11th November 1954.

12 *Sunday*

'The dragon is withered,
His bones are now crumbled;
His armour is shivered,
His splendour is humbled!'

THE HOBBIT

N·O·V·E·M·B·E·R

13 *Monday*

14 *Tuesday*

15 *Wednesday*

16 *Thursday*

17 *Friday*

18 *Saturday*

19 *Sunday*

'O proud walls! White towers! O winged crown and throne of gold!
O Gondor, Gondor! Shall Men behold the Silver Tree,
Or West Wind blow again between the Mountains and the Sea?'

THE TWO TOWERS

N·O·V·E·M·B·E·R

20 *Monday*

21 *Tuesday*

22 *Wednesday*

23 *Thursday*

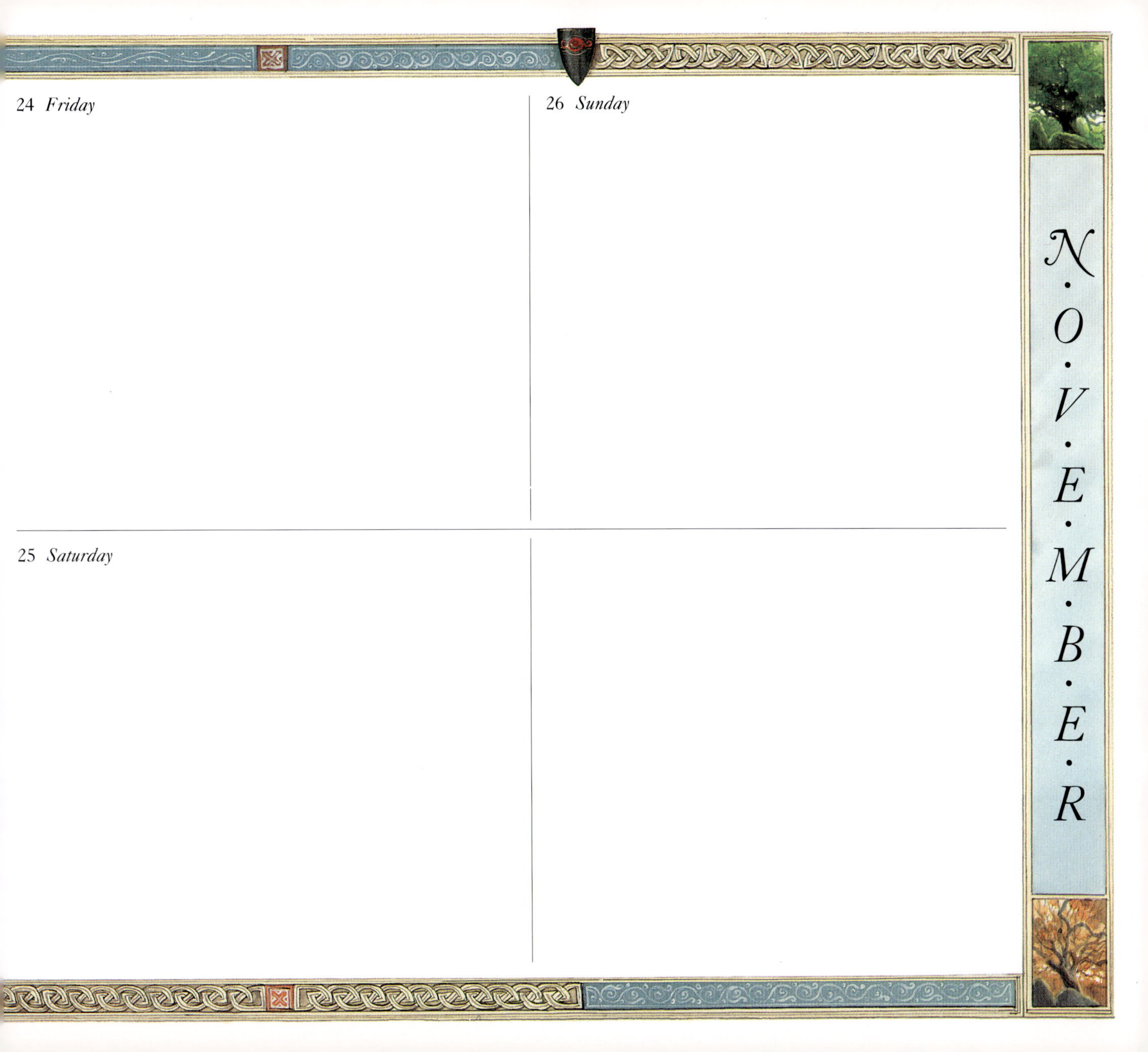

24 *Friday*

26 *Sunday*

25 *Saturday*

27 *Monday*

28 *Tuesday*

29 *Wednesday*

On 29th November 1971 Edith Tolkien died, at the age of 82.

30 *Thursday*

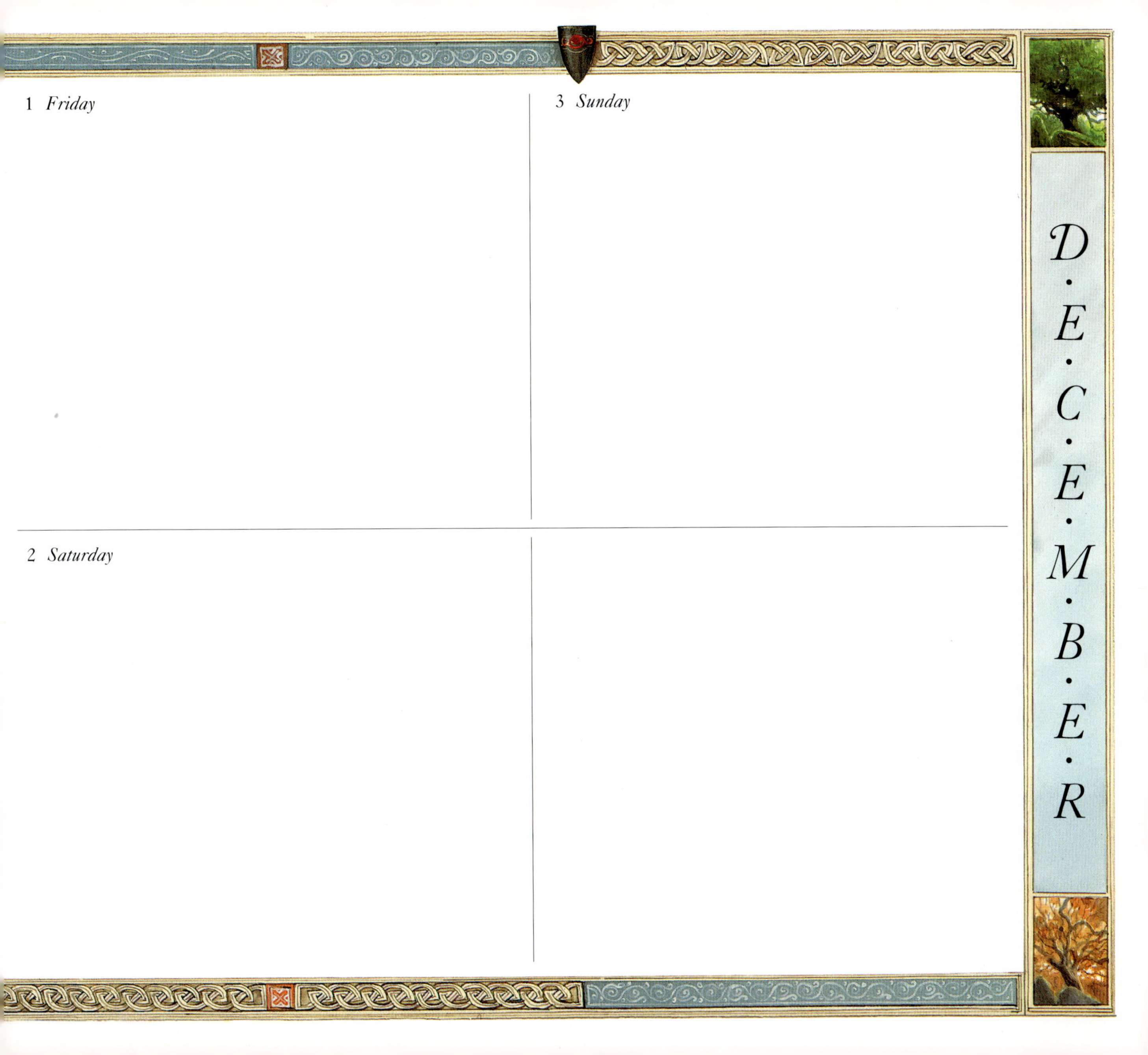

1 *Friday*

3 *Sunday*

2 *Saturday*

D·E·C·E·M·B·E·R

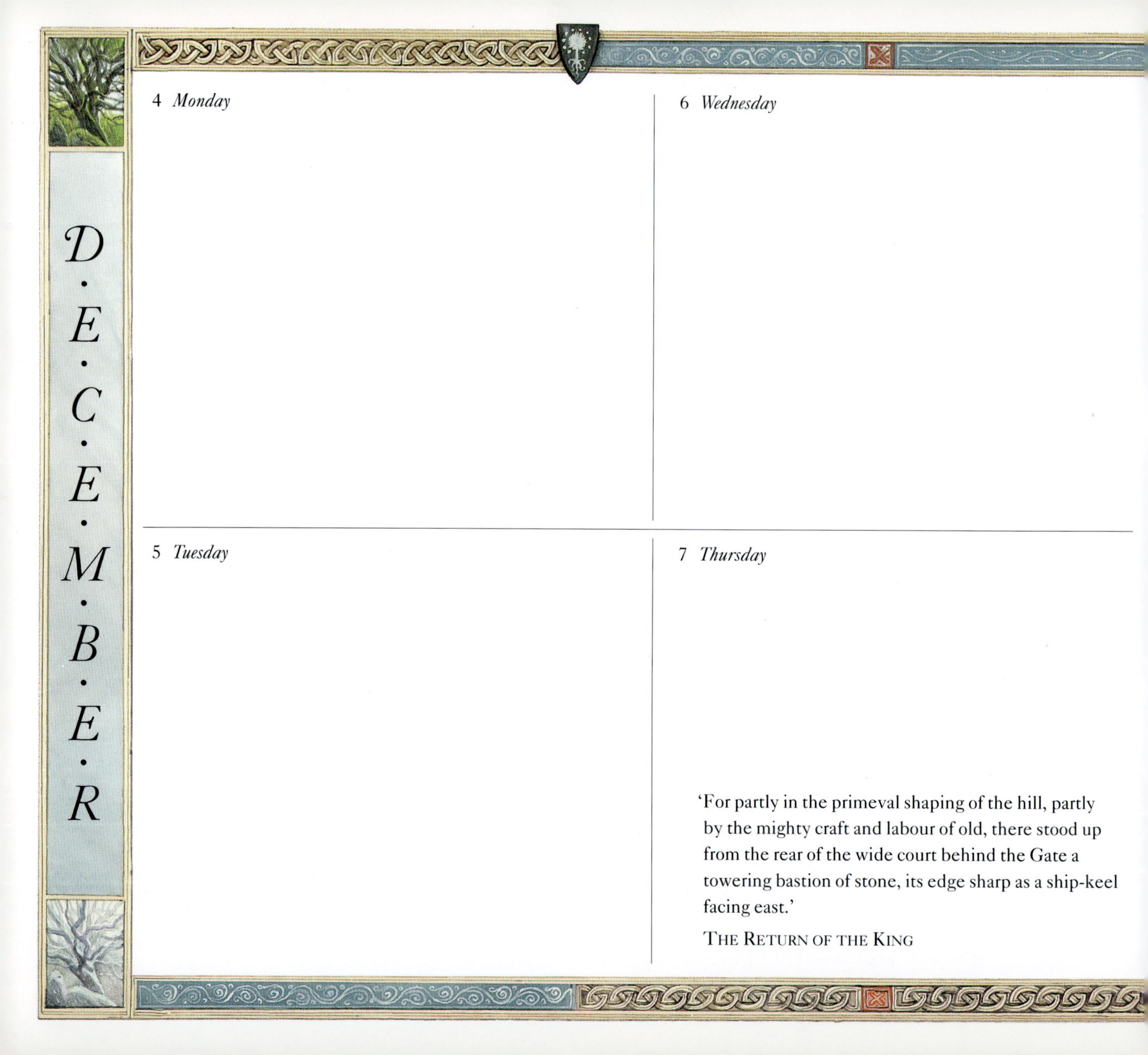

4 *Monday*

6 *Wednesday*

5 *Tuesday*

7 *Thursday*

'For partly in the primeval shaping of the hill, partly by the mighty craft and labour of old, there stood up from the rear of the wide court behind the Gate a towering bastion of stone, its edge sharp as a ship-keel facing east.'

THE RETURN OF THE KING

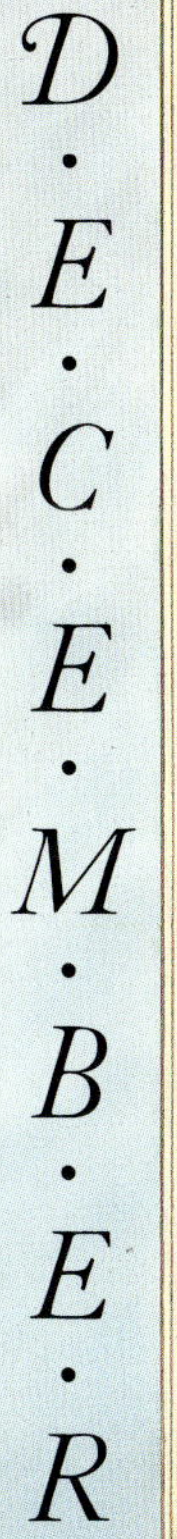
D·E·C·E·M·B·E·R

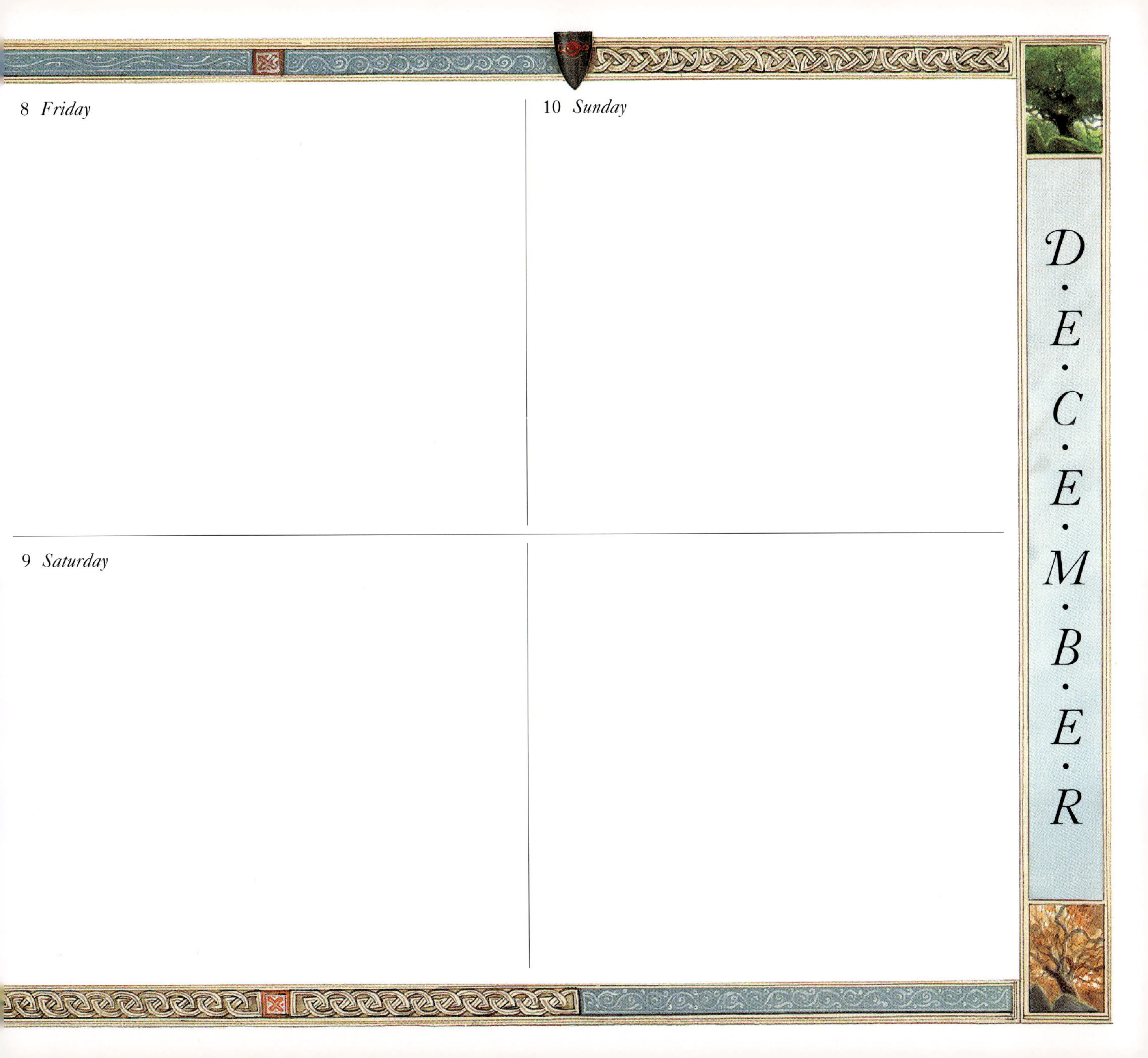

8 *Friday*

10 *Sunday*

9 *Saturday*

D·E·C·E·M·B·E·R

D·E·C·E·M·B·E·R

11 *Monday*

12 *Tuesday*

13 *Wednesday*

14 *Thursday*

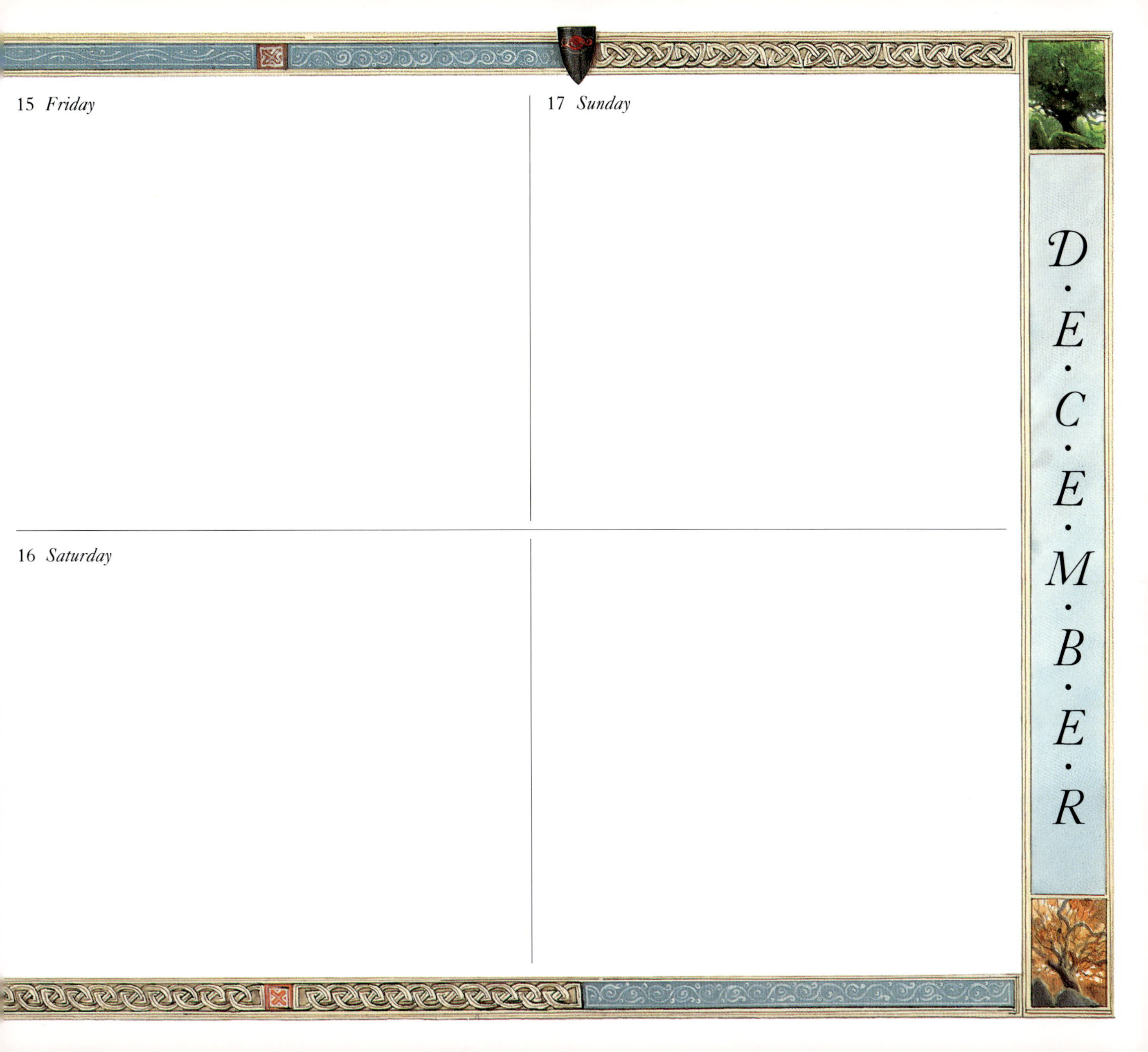

15 *Friday*

17 *Sunday*

16 *Saturday*

D·E·C·E·M·B·E·R

18 *Monday*

20 *Wednesday*

19 *Tuesday*

21 *Thursday*

22 *Friday*

24 *Sunday*

23 *Saturday*

'I sit beside the fire and think
of all that I have seen,
of meadow-flowers and butterflies
in summers that have been;
Of yellow leaves and gossamer
in autumns that there were,
with morning mist and silver sun
and wind upon my hair.'

THE FELLOWSHIP OF THE RING

D·E·C·E·M·B·E·R

25 *Monday*

26 *Tuesday*

27 *Wednesday*

28 *Thursday*

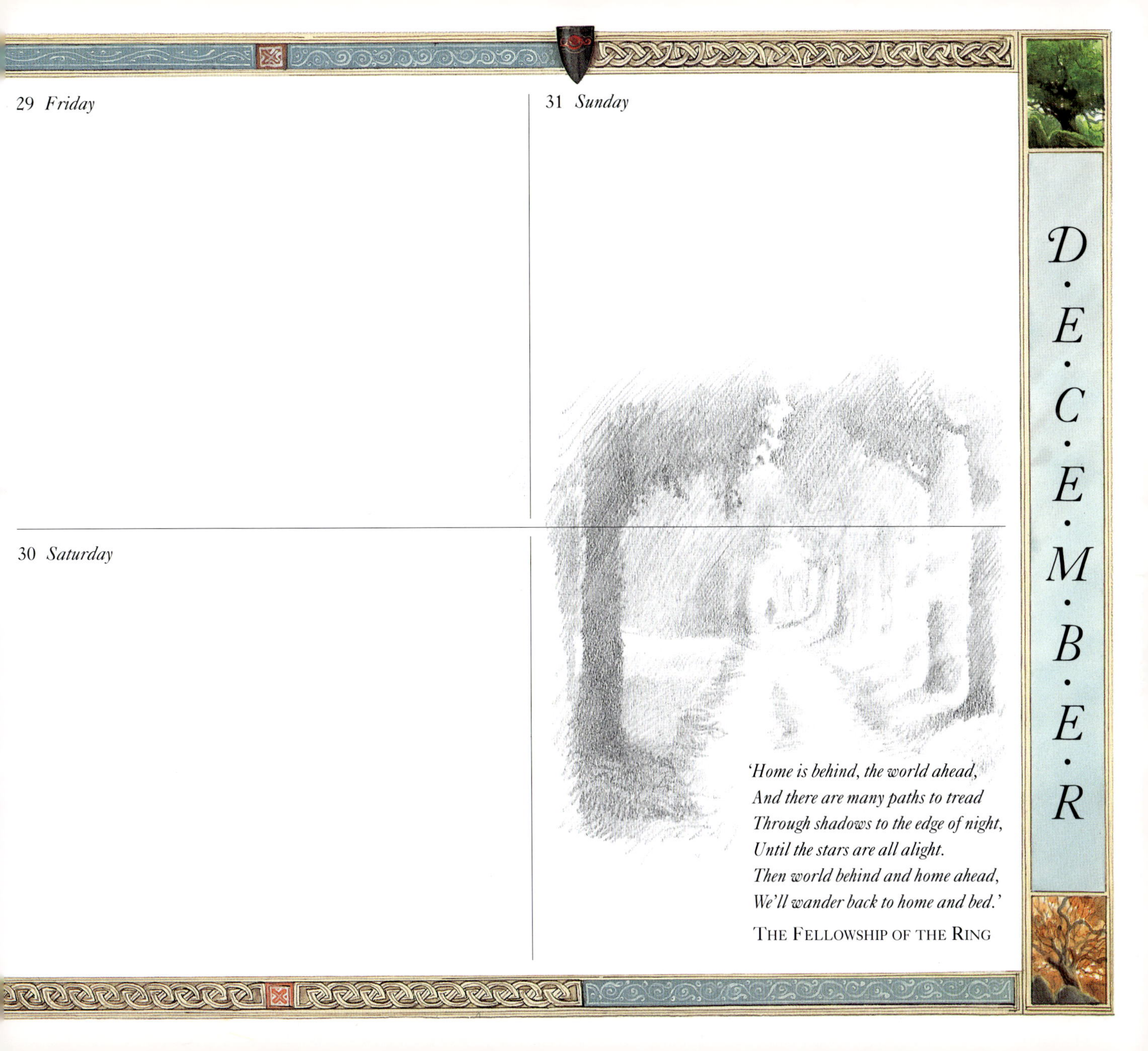

29 *Friday*

30 *Saturday*

31 *Sunday*

D·E·C·E·M·B·E·R

'Home is behind, the world ahead,
And there are many paths to tread
Through shadows to the edge of night,
Until the stars are all alight.
Then world behind and home ahead,
We'll wander back to home and bed.'

THE FELLOWSHIP OF THE RING

J·A·N·U·A·R·Y

1 *Monday*

2 *Tuesday*

3 *Wednesday*

4 *Thursday*

N·O·T·E·S